PRISONER OF THE LYCAN PRINCE

THE ROYAL LYCANS
BOOK TWO

AMY PENNZA

Prisoner of the Lycan Prince

Cover design by Miblart

CONTENT NOTICE

Please see my website for content notes so you can decide if Prisoner of the Lycan Prince is right for you.

CHAPTER ONE

EINAR

Draithmere was quiet. Just the way I liked it.

I sat at my desk, my shoulders relaxed and my gaze on the roaring fire across the room. The flames in the hearth snapped and danced, throwing shadows on the walls. Through the window, a crescent moon cast a silvery glow over the October night. Already, the air held winter's bite. But the chill was no match for Draithmere's chimneys.

The sprawling estate perched on a bluff overlooking 25,000 acres at the base of the Olympic Mountains—and every acre, tree, and blade of grass belonged to me. As far as empires went, Draithmere was modest. But I didn't need space. Unlike some people, I didn't need to feel important. No, my needs were simple. Food, forest, and fucking *quiet*.

The last commodity had been difficult to come by lately. Between running Draithmere and preventing the Puget Sound werewolf pack from terrorizing the supernatural community, my days were...noisy.

But not tonight.

Tonight, the Puget Sound alpha was dead, Draithmere was quiet, and I was going to celebrate the shit out of my solitude. The human newscasters could announce a meteor was on course to annihilate the planet, and it wouldn't disturb my peace. I'd fought Rex Addington and the rest of the Puget Sound wolves for nearly a decade. Like so many other werewolf alphas, Rex was determined to see werewolves raised above humans.

Well, *had been* determined. Past tense. The arrogant fucker was dead now, courtesy of my claws and one well-timed swipe across his throat. Hopefully, seeing their alpha's head spin across the Sound like a Frisbee was enough to deter the remaining pack members from stirring up trouble for a while. Although, knowing werewolves, Rex's death wouldn't keep them down for long.

The fire popped. Embers eddied into the air. A few spilled onto the hardwood and flared briefly before winking out.

I let a sigh fill my chest as I leaned back in my chair and stretched. As I released my breath, my worries fled with the oxygen. Addington was dead, the Puget Sound Pack was neutered, and I had an entire evening of peace and quiet on tap. No duties. No demands. Nothing was going to disturb my—

"Sir?"

I jerked my attention from the fire to the study's doorway. My steward, Arlo, stood there, a hesitant expression on his face and a manila folder held close to his chest. As he waited for me to acknowledge him, a ghostly pair of black horns flickered around his head—there and gone so quickly most people wouldn't have noticed them.

But I knew Arlo. He'd served me for fifty years. And his horns didn't come out unless he was nervous or angry.

"What is it?" I asked.

His gaze landed on the book at my elbow. "Light reading?"

In my peripheral vision, the book's cover shifted, the black leather changing to a deep, alluring red. Gold letters rearranged themselves and began to glow.

"Always," I told Arlo, ignoring the book.

Disapproval touched Arlo's eyes, but he kept his reprovals to himself as he drew a deep breath. "We have a bit of a problem, sir."

I pointed to his chest. "Is it in that folder?"

Arlo crossed to the desk and sat in one of the chairs angled in front of it. Regret swam in his dark eyes as he placed the folder on the desk's surface and slid it toward me. "Apologies, Prince Einar. I know you hoped to pass a quiet evening alone, but this is a somewhat urgent development."

I grunted as I slapped a hand on the folder and clawed it toward me. No matter how many times I told Arlo to drop my title, he insisted on maintaining a layer of formality between us. I shot him what I knew was an exasperated look as I opened the folder.

"Let's see this urgent develop—" The rest of my sentence caught in my throat as photos spilled onto my desk. Glossy and grayscale, they'd obviously been taken at night. Nevertheless, they showed their subject in startling detail. My throat went dry as I lifted the first image.

It was me, my face in profile as I unbuttoned my shirt.

The next image showed me bending to remove my jeans.

In the third photo, my body contorted as I began to shift.

The next few images showed me in various stages of transformation. The camera was ruthless and invasive, capturing my disjointed limbs and the grotesque in-between stage where pulpy organs and naked bone protruded from half-formed flesh. One frame appeared to zoom in on my face, catching my lipless grimace as my jaw lengthened into a canine snout.

In the final photo, I stood on four legs, my body fully shifted into my lycan form.

"I found the images in our post office box when I ran into town today," Arlo said. "They were sent by way of a private courier service. I already checked out the courier. It's a legitimate company. I couldn't find any ties between them and the sender." A hint of anger laced Arlo's voice. "The sender didn't attempt to hide his identity. He *wanted* us to know who he is."

"Who?" I demanded, outrage building as I met Arlo's gaze. "Who's the dead man who sent these photos?"

"Orson Ward," Arlo said. He hesitated. "Does that name mean anything to you?"

"No. Should it?"

"He's an investigative journalist. I'd never heard of him, either, but the internet says he's well-known in journalistic circles. His late wife was a respected food critic, and his family founded the oldest newspaper in Seattle. Generations of Ward family members have worked in journalism. They're like a"—Arlo groped for a word—"reporting dynasty or something."

"I don't give a fuck if they're the British royal family," I said, my voice dropping an octave. I stabbed a finger at the topmost photo. "These are threats. What does Ward want? Money?"

Arlo stared at my finger on the photo. "Sir," he said quietly.

I looked down. My finger had shifted into a claw, which now pinned the photo to the desk. With a muttered curse, I wrenched my claw from the wood and shoved the photo away. A tiny divot scarred the desk's surface. Dozens more scattered across the wood. Reminders of the other times I'd lost control and shifted unexpectedly.

"Ward wants an interview," Arlo said. With a flick of his wrist, he produced a second manila envelope—which most definitely hadn't been visible before. Arlo withdrew a single sheet of paper and placed it before me. "Forgive me, sir. I kept the letter from you so you'd have a chance to absorb the photos." Arlo avoided looking at the claw marks on the desk.

I opened my top drawer and withdrew a flask. "Probably a good idea."

Arlo's expression was neutral as he nodded toward the letter. "Ward claims he has a video of your shift, as well as footage of you killing Rex Addington. He demands that you meet him in person at his home in Seattle. If you refuse, he says he'll release the video to the media. He gives you twenty-four hours to decide."

Rage pumped hot in my veins. I uncorked the flask and took a healthy swig of its contents. The liquid burned hotter than my anger, which was exactly the point. When the fire—and the urges it brought—subsided, I set the flask aside and ran my gaze down Ward's neat, black handwriting. "He seeks to blackmail me."

"Yes, sir," Arlo murmured. "That appears to be the gist of it."

I kept reading. "He's going to release the video regardless. He claims he's being generous by allowing me to control the narrative before the rest of the world discovers werewolves are real." I huffed a humorless laugh as I met Arlo's dark stare. "Not a very good investigative journalist, is he? Cocky fucker doesn't even know the difference between werewolves and lycans."

"That's another thing," Arlo said. "Orson Ward *used* to be an acclaimed journalist. He won two Pulitzers for his reporting work. Now, he's a pariah."

"Why?" Hope fluttered at the edges of my anger. If Ward had skeletons, he was probably desperate. And desperate people were often sloppy. I could work with that.

"Three years ago," Arlo said, "someone discovered major

discrepancies in a story Ward reported. Once people started digging into his work, they realized he'd faked facts in two separate reports. When he couldn't get a scoop, Ward invented one. Then he did it again."

So I was right. Ward was desperate. On the other hand, he had photos and a video of me shifting, and he was prepared to go public. Photos were damaging enough, but a video was the sort of bite-sized content the internet loved. It would quickly go viral, racking up millions of views and, eventually, leading humans to my doorstep. Under no circumstances could I allow that to happen. The consequences were unthinkable—and deadly.

My anger stirred anew, urging me to my feet and propelling me around the desk. I stalked to the hearth and braced a hand on the stone mantel carved with snarling lycans. The fire licked higher, its heat searing my face. Orson Ward thought to blackmail me? Two could play that game.

I turned from the hearth to find Arlo standing next to his chair. His gaze was steady, his posture relaxed. Anyone meeting him for the first time would see a slight, timid-looking young man with dark hair and eyes. If they were like most people, they'd assume he was harmless. And they would be wrong.

"Tell Ward I'll meet him three days from now. He can have his interview. In the meantime, get me all the information you can find on him. I want to know everything. His family. His favorite food. Affairs. Girlfriends from high school. Assets and debts. The names of his pets. If he cares about something, I want to know about it. And then I want to talk to him face-to-face."

Arlo's gaze went to the flask on the corner of my desk. "Are you certain that's wise, sir?"

"It would be unwise to try to stop me."

He inclined his head. "I wouldn't dream of it, Your Highness."

"Glad to hear it. And you'll see to Ward?"

"I'll make sure you have all the information you require." The slightest smile touched Arlo's lips. "This won't go well for Ward, will it, sir?"

Grim anticipation spread through me. "No, old friend. It will not."

CHAPTER TWO

HARPER

Three days later

Rain streaked down the Uber's window as I stared at the passing houses. A year away hadn't dulled my memories of the neighborhood I'd grown up in. Large, stately homes with manicured lawns lined the street. The Seattle skyline rose in the distance, the buildings far enough away to allow the neighborhood's residents to claim the city without enduring its noise or traffic.

Exhaustion tugged at me, resentment following swiftly on its heels. The cheapest flight out of Chicago had required me to travel to Denver. More flights meant more anxiety, but a direct route had been out of my price range. So I'd endured a two-hour layover and frayed nerves before flying into Sea-Tac. I'd been up since 4 a.m., and I was running on caffeine, Klonopin, and the bagel I'd shoved in my face somewhere over the Midwest. Now, it was pushing dinnertime, and I still didn't know why my father insisted on me returning home.

His text three days ago had been frustratingly vague, saying only that he'd "stumbled across something remarkable" and needed my help. When I pushed back, he reminded me that my tuition came out of my mother's meager trust—which he administered. The threat was clear: fly to Seattle or expect to spend my last semester at Northwestern scrambling to afford books, classes, and a dozen other expenses. I was seven months away from a degree that would let me earn my own livelihood. And now my father dangled my freedom before me like a carrot on a stick.

The Uber driver slowed, squinting at the faded numbers on a mailbox.

"It's this one," I said.

The man grunted, then pulled into the driveway that led to my childhood home. "Nice place," he said as we passed through the open, wrought iron gate flanked by brick pillars.

"Thanks." As soon as I said it, I bit my lip. The house wasn't mine. Undoubtedly, the driver knew it simply by looking at me —and the battered backpack I'd taken on the plane. But the house wasn't nice, either. It was pleasing enough from the road, but a closer look revealed neglect. And the driver had no way of knowing the gate was open because it rusted in place years ago.

The house's true condition became more apparent as we progressed up the drive. Hedges that were once bright green and trimmed into geometrical shapes were now brown and lopsided. Cracks had formed in the driveway, and grass burst through the crevices. The paint on the two-tiered fountain was flaking, revealing the fiberglass underneath. When I was eight, my parents filled it with champagne the night my father won his first Pulitzer. Now, the fountain was dry, its lower bowl littered with dead leaves.

The driver stopped in the half-circle drive in front of the house's previously glossy black double doors.

"Thanks for the ride," I said, grabbing my backpack.

"No problem." He hesitated, his gaze on the house. "You, uh, sure you want to go in there alone?"

"Yes, it's fine. It's my parents' house." I slipped from the car and made my way to the steps. One of the brass door knockers was missing. The other looked ready to abandon its post and join its companion.

The doors weren't locked, and I stepped into the darkened foyer.

"Dad?" The foyer was empty, the glass chandelier suspended above black-and-white tiles covered in shadow. On a distant wall, a brighter square of wallpaper marked where my mother's curio cabinet had once stood. Memories swept me, transporting me back to a time when the cabinet had gleamed with fresh polish and the interior shelves had boasted dozens of the miniature glass vases my mother loved to collect. She'd been thrilled to find a local glassblower who repaired some of the damaged pieces she'd bought because she liked them too much to pass them over. On one occasion, she showed me a delicate Tiffany vase with a restored handle.

"Look, Harper, you can't even tell it was broken. The whole piece is stronger now. And the glassblower found an additional crack when he was working. So, in a way, maybe it was a good thing the handle was broken."

The vase—and the cabinet—were long gone now, nothing but the square on the wallpaper to prove they ever existed. The pattern repeated around the room, the more vivid spaces in the paper like tombstones in a furniture graveyard. In the beginning, I thought my father sold my mother's things because he couldn't bear to be reminded of what he'd lost.

Then I discovered the truth.

Drawing a deep breath, I moved deeper into the house. "Dad? It's me."

No response. But my father was expecting me. And it wasn't like he had anywhere else to be. Not anymore. Not for the last three years.

Tightening my grip on my backpack strap, I left the foyer and followed the long hallway that led to the kitchen. After a few more steps, the smell of garbage and sour milk hit my nose. When I entered the kitchen, the stench of rot made my stomach do a sickening flip. Dirty dishes filled the sink under the window. Bags of chips, half-filled cereal bowls, and boxes of snack cakes littered the counter. A fly trap dangled from a push pin thrust into the drywall, its long, yellow ribbon covered in dead flies.

My heart sped up, and dread settled around my shoulders. My father had always tended toward absentmindedness, especially when he was working. But this was different. The kitchen was filthy. And the house was so quiet. It was almost as if...

I sucked in a breath. What if Dad was—?

A clicking sound interrupted my spiraling thoughts. Heart racing, I followed the sound to the empty dining room, where I paused to exhale in relief as the noise turned into the telltale clatter of a computer keyboard. The keystrokes didn't slow as I made my way to my father's office in the back of the house. His door was cracked, revealing Dad seated at his desk and bent over his laptop.

His silvery hair stood up in a dozen different directions, giving him the look of a man who'd wandered into a cloud. A pair of glasses balanced just above the tip of his nose. He held his tongue between his teeth as he typed, his fingers flying. Weak daylight streamed through the windows and fell over him in watery shafts.

I hesitated, my hand raised to knock, when he looked up.

"Harper!" His face split in a grin, showing the gap between his front teeth. "Come in, come in! I'm on a deadline, but I can break for a bit."

Confusion gripped me as I stepped into the office. *I'm on a deadline.* I'd heard it often enough over the years.

"Sorry I can't come to your soccer game, honey. I'm on a deadline."

"I'll be a few hours late. I'm on a deadline."

"I'm on a deadline, so I'll have to miss your choir concert. Next time, okay?"

My father's deadlines had always come between us. But he shouldn't have a deadline right now. He hadn't worked in three years.

Images from the kitchen rose in my mind. Oh god, what if he was losing it? His scandals had finally broken him, and now he was "working" on his computer, probably typing nonsense. Should I call someone? I shifted my backpack higher on my shoulder. My phone was tucked in a side pocket. If he became suspicious or combative, I could step outside and call for help. But who would I call? And how would I pay for it?

My father beckoned me forward. "Don't just stand by the door! I need another set of eyes on this."

I drifted closer, more resentment brewing. If he'd forced me out of my classes and onto a plane so I could *edit* for him, I was going to lose my everloving shit. "What are you working on?"

He leaned forward in his chair, an aura of excitement hovering around him. "The biggest scoop of my life. You're not going to believe this story. It's going to turn things around for us, Harper."

Doubtful. There was no coming back from what he'd done. Manufacturing evidence about one country selling nuclear weapons to another—and accusing US government officials of being party to the scheme—was the career equivalent of pouring gasoline over a forest fire. My father was lucky he wasn't in prison.

I stopped in front of his desk, my hand tight on my backpack strap. "What kind of story is it?"

"Sit, sit," he said, gesturing to one of the folding metal lawn chairs that had replaced the tufted leather set. "This is the sort of thing you really need to see to appreciate." He gave me a conspiratorial wink as he flipped his laptop around. "Luckily, I've got everything on video. Prepare to be stunned."

"All right." I heard the wariness in my voice as I lowered my backpack to the ground and sat. A fresh spike of irritation prompted me to add, "I can't wait."

If my father heard the sarcasm, he didn't show it. His eagerness was palpable as he pulled up a video player. With a final, bright-eyed glance at me, he clicked *play*.

A tall, powerful-looking man filled the screen. The video, which bore my father's name as a watermark in the lower left corner, had been taken at night in what appeared to be a forest. The footage was soundless, and the image was bleached of color. But a full moon bathed the man's face and body in bold light.

The video zoomed in, capturing the man's features in more detail. His eyes were gray...no, silver. And they appeared to glow.

Against my will, I leaned forward. The man was handsome, with rugged features and dark blond hair. But his looks alone didn't draw me. No, something else about him held my attention. I'd covered enough plays and music festivals as a student journalist to know what it was. He had a certain presence, like a movie star or stage actor who owns a scene regardless of the script. This man would attract attention in baggy sweatpants in the middle of a grocery store.

On screen, he lowered his head and began unbuttoning his shirt.

I jerked my gaze to my father's. "Dad—"

"Shh, shh," he said, not looking away from the laptop. "It's all right. Keep watching."

The man dropped his shirt, then reached for the fastening of his jeans.

"Oh my god—"

"Harper, it's *fine*."

"He's stripping!" And my face was on fire. At the same time, disbelief swept me. My father had coerced me into traveling two thousand miles so we could watch homemade porn together. I shot to my feet, one hand reaching for my backpack.

Nude now, the man began to...*change*.

I froze, one hand still extended toward the ground.

The man's skin rippled. Then his whole body rippled. Waves of muscle and bone moved in ways they absolutely should not have been able to move. After a second, the man dropped to his hands and knees.

And I forgot about his nudity. Now, my heart thumped painfully as the man's limbs lengthened. Hair rushed over his skin like a video in fast forward. Only this footage wasn't sped up. The trees in the background continued moving normally, the branches swaying in a light breeze.

The man's face elongated, forming a snout like a...

No.

The video was doctored. Some kind of editing trick my father had cooked up. Because there was no way I'd just watched a man transform into a werewolf.

The animal lifted its head, and a pair of bright golden eyes gleamed like car headlights.

"Keep watching," my father said. "There's a time jump because I followed him down the beach."

"What? Where?"

"Puget Sound." Dad pointed to the screen. "Here. He's going to attack the other one."

The video flickered, and the scene changed to a moonlit beach. A moment later, the same massive, buff-colored wolf from the first part of the video streaked down the sand and launched itself at a clump of shadows. Except the shadows weren't shadows at all. As the wolf tumbled across the beach, I realized it grappled with a second wolf. My heart thumped painfully as the fight unfolded. Once again, there was no sound, but this time I was grateful for it. Blood sprayed the sand as the wolves slashed and bit at each other. The second wolf was smaller, with shaggy black fur. It was obviously fighting for its life.

"What is this?" I asked, my voice hoarse as a sense of doom slipped around me. The video couldn't be real. Clearly, my father had used some kind of editing software. But it wasn't like him. The video quality was too good for my father's woeful tech skills. He had a hard time remembering his Facebook login.

"Almost done," he said. "This is the best part."

On the screen, the smaller wolf lunged at the larger wolf. The larger wolf spun away, moving so quickly its body blurred. The next second, the smaller wolf sprawled on the sand, its head severed from its body. Blood pumped from the stump of its neck, the color black in the moonlight. The video stopped, freezing on a frame of the buff-colored wolf standing over the black wolf's decapitated body.

Nausea burned my throat. My knees loosened, and I sat heavily in my chair, making the metal squeak in protest.

My father's expression was triumphant. "Do you see what I mean now?" He gestured to the screen. "Every news outlet in the world is going to be clamoring for this."

I shook my head. "I don't get it. How did you make this?"

Dad's salt-and-pepper eyebrows lifted. "I didn't *make* it, Harper. I recorded it as it happened. Everything you just saw is one hundred percent real. This is definitive proof that werewolves exist. It's going to change the world. That's why I wanted you home. Once this story breaks, our lives are never going to be the same."

For a second, I could only stare at him. Then I made my tone as gentle as possible. "Dad, I know you still miss Mom. Have you been, um, taking anything?"

"You mean like drugs?" His gaze sharpened, the air of excitement giving way to an intensity that pinned me to my chair. Suddenly, he was the Orson Ward of old. Pulitzer Prize winner. Renowned reporter who'd broken major stories on six continents. The investigative journalist courted by *The New York Times* and a dozen other newspapers. But no one had ever been able to tempt him to leave the *Sentinel*. No matter how many accolades he earned, he'd stayed loyal to our family's paper.

My father gave me the stare that had cowed dictators and corrupt captains of industry. "To answer your question, no, I'm not on drugs or any other kind of mind-altering substance."

I cleared my throat. "I didn't mean—"

"I know this footage is difficult to believe." My father flashed a rueful smile. "Considering what happened in the past, I can't blame you for doubting me. But the video is real." He leaned over his desk again. "This is on level with an alien invasion, Harper. Once the world finds out werewolves live among us, people are going to have questions. I'm going to give them answers."

Silence fell, the only sound the patter of rain on the windows. He seemed so sure of himself. The video was obviously fake, but there was no question *he* believed it. "How will you do that?" I asked. "Give answers, I mean."

Dad's gaze didn't waver. "I'm going to interview the werewolf in the video. He'll be here in about an hour."

The distant slam of a door split the air. Dad frowned, his gaze shooting to the office's doorway. Alarm shot through me, and I craned my head, following my father's gaze. Heavy footfalls rang out.

I stood so quickly the lawn chair rocked backward and almost tipped before settling. I whipped my head toward my father. "What's going on?"

The footfalls grew louder. Closer. Dad rose, then backed away from his desk. My throat went dry, and my heart galloped in my chest. I looked around for a weapon, but the office was empty except for my father's desk and the lawn chairs.

My father stared at the door, his face as ashen as the sky outside. "I... I don't..."

A tall, muscular man strode through the door. My jaw dropped as I took in dark blond hair and ruggedly handsome features. Broad shoulders and piercing silver eyes.

But they'd turned gold when he shifted in the video.

The man stalked forward, vaulted over my father's desk, and gripped him around the throat. My scream bounced off the walls as I stumbled backward. My foot caught the side of my backpack, and I stumbled again before catching myself.

Phone. I had to get to my phone. I started forward—

"I wouldn't, Miss Ward," a second man said as he stepped into the room. Lean and dark-haired, he looked about my age. He stopped in the center of the office and folded his hands at his waist. Despite the threat in his words, his face was kind, and his expression was almost apologetic as he added, "Prince Einar prefers to handle this without bloodshed."

My father made a gurgling sound as the man from the video lifted him by the throat and slammed him against the wall where a bookcase had once stood. Large windows on either side showed the rain coming down harder outside.

"Stop!" I screamed, moving around the desk. "He's"—I searched for a way to make the man stop his attack—"he has a heart condition."

The man, who was apparently called Einar, turned his head and met my gaze. His nostrils flared, almost as if he scented the air. After a beat, his silver eyes narrowed. "Well, that's a lie." He turned back to my father. "Dishonesty runs in the family. How charming."

Red crept up my father's face as he clawed at the man's wrist. "Let...me...go..." He dug his fingernails into Einar's skin, leaving bloody furrows.

Einar grunted. A second later, buff-colored fur rushed over his hand. Between one breath and the next, his arm transformed into an overly large wolf's paw with long, black claws. Einar leaned forward, and the claws sank into my father's throat.

"No!" I started forward, only to be brought up short by a hand around my bicep. The young man hauled me back, his grip surprisingly solid. We were the same height and possibly the same weight, but he was obviously much stronger than he looked.

"Stay out of this, Miss Ward," he said. "Prince Einar doesn't want anyone to get hurt."

Prince?

"You play a dangerous game trying to blackmail me," Einar told my father. "You want an interview? Fine. Let's have one." He pulled my father off the wall, carried him to the desk chair, and slammed him into it. Immediately, my father curled over the desktop, gasping and coughing.

Einar looked at me, then pointed to one of the lawn chairs. "Sit."

Before I could respond, the dark-haired man propelled me to the chair and pushed me into it. Einar snagged the other chair, positioned it in front of my father's desk, and sat. The metal groaned but held his weight. He lifted his paw, examining it as if he found it interesting. Slowly, it slid back into a human hand.

My heart tried to pound from my chest. *I'm hallucinating.* It was the only explanation that made sense. Maybe the pharmacy had messed up my medication, and I was in the throes of some kind of weird, trippy side effect.

Einar focused on my father. "Look at me, Ward."

Gasping, my father lifted his head. The movement was jerky, like he was a marionette on a string. By some miracle, his glasses still clung to his face. Capillaries had burst in his eyes, and the whites were smeared with red.

"That's better," Einar said. His tone was conversational, as if he'd popped by for tea. He settled more deeply in his lawn chair, his body dwarfing the flimsy metal frame. "Arlo, please show Mr. Ward the terms."

The younger man stepped forward, producing a bundle of papers from somewhere. He placed them on the desk in front of my father, then pulled a fountain pen from his pocket and set it next to the paperwork.

"Now," Einar said, "here's how this is going to work. You took footage and photos of me without my consent. I'm here to take those things back." He made a regal gesture in Arlo's direction, and the younger man sprang forward and seized my father's laptop.

My father made a pained noise, but kept his mouth shut.

Einar continued. "I assume you've made copies of your materials and squirreled them away in all kinds of places.

Regretfully, I don't trust you to hand everything over. So I'll be taking your daughter with me to incentivize your cooperation."

"What?" I gasped. He couldn't be serious. I looked at my father. "Dad?"

"My terms are spelled out clearly in the contract," Einar said as if I hadn't spoken. "Miss Ward will live under my protection until I'm satisfied you've returned every scrap and shred of my likeness, along with whatever story you were writing." Einar's voice went low. "And let me be plain. If you ever attempt to write about me or my kind again, neither you nor your daughter will enjoy what happens afterward."

Fear gripped me. What was he saying?

My father paled. "You won't hurt her," he rasped, his voice hoarse.

"That's up to you," Einar said. He nodded toward the contract. "Honor the agreement, and you'll have nothing to worry about."

My father looked down at the papers in front of him. Slowly, he reached out and pulled the contract toward him.

"Dad!" I came out of my chair, outrage searing my veins. "Are you actually considering this?" I swung my gaze to Einar. "You can't take me with you. I won't go."

He frowned. "You're not a party to these negotiations, Miss Ward. I don't require your acquiescence."

"I'm making myself a party!"

"That's not how contract law works."

"I—" Wait, was I really arguing the ins and outs of contracts with him?

Einar turned to my father. "One more thing. Page twelve. If you don't sign, I'll be forced to go public with how you fabricated the details for that story you did about the President of the Hartling Foundation."

The blood drained from my father's face.

Disappointment washed through me in a sickening wave. The Hartling story was a highlight of his career—and one of the pieces that earned him a Pulitzer. A beloved philanthropist had spent a decade siphoning money from a charity he founded. My father's reporting exposed him as a fraud more interested in rubbing elbows with celebrities than helping people. The scandal had spanned several countries and implicated a number of government officials.

"Dad," I said, hearing the censure in my voice. "The President of the Hartling Foundation went to jail over that."

My father swallowed. "He did all the things he was accused of. I just...supplemented with some quotes."

"Quotes no one ever actually spoke," Einar said. "Apparently, inventing sources is frowned upon in journalism." He smiled. "I've learned quite a bit about journalistic malpractice over the past few days. It's been very eye-opening."

Anger warred with disappointment in my gut. My whole life, I'd looked up to my father as someone who held the powerful accountable. His misdeeds had cost our family its legacy. The name Ward had meant something once. Now it was a cautionary tale. An embarrassing footnote.

Dad met Einar's gaze. "I'll give you all the files. I swear it. There's no need to involve Harper in this."

Einar's smile didn't reach his eyes. "That would be acceptable if I could take you at your word. But we both know that's not the case." He stood, looming over the desk. "So your daughter will be coming with me."

"No," I said, my heart in my throat. "Dad, this is crazy. You can't hand me over to a stranger like a piece of furniture!"

His expression was stark. Suddenly, he seemed diminished, his body too frail for his fifty-four years. "I don't have a choice."

"Yes, you do!"

"But the Hartling story—"

"Who cares? Things can't get any worse!"

My father hesitated.

"Should we discuss the other stories?" Einar asked.

"Others?" I demanded, my voice approaching a screech.

Einar folded his arms. "Pages fourteen through twenty-seven." When I glared at him, he gave me a mild look. "You'll find I'm very thorough."

My father picked up the pen.

"Dad!" My heart tried to pound from my chest. "He could abuse me. Assault me. Hurt me in ways a man hurts a woman."

"Absolutely not," Einar snapped, his voice like a whip. "I don't touch unwilling females."

I channeled all the hate I could muster into my stare. "I assure you, I am *very* unwilling. In all ways."

He shrugged.

"I'm sorry, Harper," my father whispered.

Disorientation swept me. This wasn't happening. I swung toward the door. Arlo stood in my path, his dark eyes steady.

My father flipped to the last page.

"Dad," I rasped, cold creeping through my veins.

With a shaking hand, he signed his name.

Einar stepped forward, pulled the contract toward him, and flipped it around. He leaned over the desk and gave my father a pointed look. "Pen."

"Oh," my father said, startling. He extended the pen. "Sorry."

The sense of surreality increased. Numbness spread through me as I watched Einar scrawl his name on the line next to my father's signature.

Einar Rothkilde.

My new owner. Nausea twisted my gut.

Einar looked at me. "In a house like this, I assume your

bedroom is upstairs. Arlo will accompany you to gather your things."

I drew myself up. "I—"

"If you're not back downstairs within five minutes, I'll come fetch you. That would be a bad way to begin our arrangement, Miss Ward." His smile returned. "So I suggest you hurry."

CHAPTER THREE

HARPER

For the second time in under an hour, I sat in the back of a car while rain streaked the window. This time, however, I wasn't alone.

Einar sat across from me in a full manspread, his big, obnoxious body taking up the entire bench seat. Just my luck, the seat faced mine, and a thick pane of privacy glass sealed us in the cabin.

He didn't appear the least bit concerned as he stretched an arm along the back of his seat, making his button-down mold to his thick chest. He seemed even bigger in the car. At five-seven, I was taller than average for a woman. But he had at least eight inches on me. Maybe more. Unlike Arlo, who'd slid into the driver's seat the second we stepped outside, Einar filled out every single one of those inches with solid muscle.

Fortunately, there was enough distance between us to ensure his knees didn't brush mine. I'd been poor for a while, but I grew up with money, and I knew the Mercedes-Maybach didn't come cheap. A man with a personal assistant, a half-million-dollar car, and the nerve to kidnap women by way of contract probably didn't get told "no" very often. But if I was going to survive this, I needed to set some ground rules. Like now.

"You can't keep me prisoner," I said.

One dirty blond eyebrow went up. Einar removed his arm from the back of the seat. I tensed, but he merely reached into his front pocket, withdrew a metal flask, and unscrewed it. Outside, the scenery whipped by more quickly as we merged onto the highway. Einar tipped the flask back, his golden throat working as he took a generous pull. He lowered it with a breathy, irritating "ahh" before spinning the cap back on and tucking the flask in his pocket. When he finished, he slung his arm along the seat again and looked out the window.

Great. I'd been kidnapped by an asshole billionaire who was also a drunk. And...huge.

I gnawed at my bottom lip. He'd said he wouldn't hurt me. In fact, he'd sounded offended at the mere suggestion. So that meant he had no intention of me sharing his bed. Right?

Nerves prickled down my spine. My backpack rested at my feet. Moving it wouldn't help anything. But what if I didn't move it? My heart rate picked up.

On the other hand, moving it wouldn't *hurt* anything.

Glancing down, I used my foot to nudge the logo facing outward. Einar still gazed out the window. "Did you hear what I said?" I asked.

He looked at me, his eyes the same color as the rain-drenched sky outside. "Remind me."

I clenched my fists in my lap. "I said you can't keep me prisoner."

"It appears I'm doing just that." He nodded toward the door. "Unless you think you can survive a tumble from a car going seventy miles per hour. Besides, I have a signed contract."

"Illegal clauses in contracts are unenforceable."

He lifted his hand from the back of the seat. "The clause isn't illegal in my world, Miss Ward."

My stomach did a weird flip. Something about the way he said my name made me want to squirm in my seat. Which was almost as ridiculous as him thinking a signed contract gave him the right to abduct me. Against my will, I focused on his hand—the hand that had looked like a *very convincing* animal paw. But that was impossible. I drew a deep breath. This guy was obviously a jerk. But he had to possess at least a modicum of humanity, didn't he? Few people were completely unredeemable.

"My father has done some terrible things," I said. "He lied about people for his own gain. I make no excuses for him. But he took my mother's death hard. I don't want to speculate about his mental state, but he's obviously experiencing some kind of mental break. Whatever he did to you, it's not right for you to play into this idea that he captured you transforming into a werewolf."

"I didn't transform into a werewolf."

Thank god. If Einar was going to be rational, we could—

"I transformed into a lycan. The differences between werewolves and lycans couldn't be more glaring, so I'd appreciate it if you didn't slander me that way again."

Frustration rose. How long was he going to keep this up? Maybe he was one of those bored rich men who played elaborate role-playing games.

If so, maybe there was a story there. Who better to cover it than a reporter embedded, albeit reluctantly, in his life? If I could get him talking, maybe I could forge a connection with him. Make him see me as a person instead of a bargaining chip. Someone he could commiserate with. Like Clarice in *Silence of the Lambs.*

Okay, maybe that was a bad example.

I forced my shoulders to relax. "What are the differences?"

Einar studied me, intelligence burning in his eyes. Whatever else he was, he wasn't stupid. He'd also clearly done his homework on my father, which meant he'd almost certainly dug into my background, too. He had to know I was months away from a journalism degree.

Damn. This wasn't going to work. And now I'd just reminded him I was Orson Ward's daughter.

"Lycans are born," he said. "Werewolves are made."

My heart leapt, and curiosity sparked despite my shitty circumstances. "So, lycans make werewolves?"

"No. Werewolves make werewolves. Their origins are murky, but our lore says that an ancient human king once ruled a vast and prosperous kingdom. He had everything. Castles, gold, and a beautiful queen. His army was full of noble knights. The king was unaware that one of these knights happened to be a lycan."

Outside, the sky had darkened. Rain lashed the windows. I leaned forward. "This knight could transform into a wolf?"

"A *lycan*," Einar said with another lift of his brow. "We're bigger and faster than werewolves. We also live longer."

"How—?"

"Five hundred years, give or take. The maximum werewolf lifespan is three hundred years, but most wolves die in petty dominance contests before they get that far."

Oh, he was really laying it on thick. Fine, I could play along. "How old are you?"

"One hundred and fifty-two. Lycans age slowly."

Right. I let my gaze wander over his unlined face and the thick hair pushed back from a smooth forehead. His claw stunt in my father's office was obviously a trick. A man who owned a Maybach could afford Hollywood-level prosthetics. He'd

conned my father, and now he was carrying out some sort of revenge plot. Nevertheless, the hair on my nape lifted as I cleared my throat.

"Okay. So, what happened with the knight?"

Einar's gaze was steady, as if he didn't care whether I believed him. "Tale as old as time. He fell in love with the queen. They carried on for decades, conducting an affair in secret. But she got old, as humans do. The knight turned out to be a bit of a fool, and he bit her, breaking one of our most sacred laws on the nonexistent chance she would rise again as a lycan. He waited for her to die."

"But she didn't," I guessed.

"Nope. She turned, becoming the first werewolf. The knight created an abomination, mixing lycan blood with human."

Something within me bristled. "That's...elitist."

"Spoken like someone who's never faced off with a werewolf. The world is full of monsters, Miss Ward, including those that should have never been made. I believe Mary Shelley wrote about it. Or do they not teach *Frankenstein* at Northwestern?" The ghost of a smile touched his lips. "Perhaps it's too elitist for the curriculum."

I couldn't keep the edge of anger from my voice. "The monster in that story spent his life trying to help and befriend humans who always turned against him."

"He also killed several of them. I promise you, no werewolf you encountered would seek to help or befriend you."

"So far, werewolves sound exactly like lycans."

Waning sunlight made his eyes appear brighter. "I'm relieved to know you're familiar with the story. The state of higher education these days makes me worry for the future."

It was an effort not to grind my molars together. "Did the knight and the queen live happily ever after?"

"Not in the slightest. The shift restored the queen to her former youth and beauty. The king, who was ill and dying, demanded to know how she'd managed it. As his suspicions grew, he noticed the knight never appeared to age, either. It didn't take much for the king to put two and two together. When the queen denied an affair, the king tortured a confession from her. Once the king learned the truth, he forced the queen to bite him. Men are far more likely to survive a werewolf's bite, although the virus tends to favor the assholes of the world. The king was, as you've probably surmised, an accomplished asshole, and he turned, becoming the second werewolf to ever live. Then he killed his wife for cuckolding him."

My breath hitched. *Cuckolding* was an unusual word. An old word. Something someone born in the 1800s might say. I shoved that thought away before it could take root.

"What happened to the knight?" I asked.

"No one knows. The story says he disappeared."

"And the king?"

"He swore a blood oath to seek revenge for the shame his queen brought upon the kingdom. According to the lore, he bit the rest of his knights, turning them one by one to create an entire army of werewolves. They spread throughout the kingdom and beyond, making others just like them. And they inherited the king's rage and thirst for vengeance. Lycans and werewolves have been at war ever since."

Outside, the sun slipped below the horizon, surrendering to the October gloom. The rain continued, leaving phantom trails on the windows. Einar pulled out his flask and took another healthy swig.

I bit the inside of my cheek, wavering between keeping my mouth shut and asking the obvious question. *Oh, to hell with it.*

"Do you always drink alcohol during the day?"

He tucked the flask into his pocket and gave me a level look. "No."

End of discussion. I'd conducted enough interviews to know when a subject didn't want to elaborate. Okay, so perhaps a different angle.

"Your servant called you a prince."

"Arlo is my steward, not my servant. And, yes, he uses my title."

The car, the contract, the hyper-realistic claw hand. Einar's accent was American, but that didn't necessarily mean anything. Plenty of European countries had princes running around the globe.

"If you're a prince," I said, "that implies you're the son of a king."

His chest lifted as he stretched his other arm along the seat. He was tall enough for the position to be comfortable instead of awkward. He exhaled on a sigh. "That's usually how these things work, yes."

"So your father is the king?"

"No."

Now, I *did* take a second to clench my jaw. "Your uncle?"

"My brother is king of all lycans. And that's enough questions for now, Miss Ward."

Instant tension arced between us. The car's engine purred as we continued to race toward some unknown destination. The sun was long gone, but Einar's eyes still shone so brightly they didn't seem real. *Or human,* a little voice whispered in my mind.

I squeezed my hands together in my lap. "Where are you taking me?"

"That's another question." He withdrew his flask and drank again. A bead of clear liquid clung to his bottom lip. He rubbed it away with his thumb.

I looked down at my hands, where I'd dug my nails into my palm, leaving little half-moons in my skin.

"Draithmere," Einar said, bringing my head back up. As I realized he'd answered my question, he pocketed the flask and turned his gaze to the darkness beyond the window. "It's the name of my home—and yours for the foreseeable future."

CHAPTER FOUR

EINAR

Harper was quiet for the rest of the drive, but I could almost see the gears turning behind her big blue eyes.

She sneaked glances at me, undoubtedly taking my measure. Trying to figure me out. When the drive stretched for two hours, she twisted her fingers in her lap, her body vibrating with anxiety. I waited for her questions to start up again—or for the light smattering of freckles across the bridge of her nose to crinkle as she demanded I release her. But she said nothing.

Which was...well, it would be ridiculous to call it disappointing. Because I wasn't disappointed. She was a busybody reporter just like her father, and she'd obviously decided to try to crack me open and read me like a book. I'd given her enough material to let her think I was a willing participant in her scheme.

But I preferred her silence. I certainly didn't need to hear her husky voice again, or to see her gnaw at her plump lower lip when she was thinking. I didn't need to notice the swells of her full breasts lifting under her gray sweater when she sighed in obvious exasperation. I didn't need to inhale slowly, catching the notes of vanilla and honeysuckle in whatever perfume she wore.

And I didn't need to wonder why she continuously nudged her beaten-up backpack with her foot when she thought I wasn't looking. I couldn't afford to be curious about the woman I'd taken. If I was honest with myself, I shouldn't have taken her. I'd resisted the idea, recognizing it for the folly it was. But Orson Ward owned nothing of value. Arlo had left no stone unturned, and the reports he'd presented painted a stark portrait of Ward's finances. The man was within weeks of complete financial ruin. Harper was the only thing Orson had left in the world. So I'd taken her.

When we arrived at Draithmere, I was going to send her to her room, order Arlo to keep her out of trouble, and then put her out of my mind until I was satisfied her father had turned over all the evidence of my shift. But with a weasel like Orson Ward, I'd have to be careful. And that could take a while.

Fucking Orson Ward. I didn't have time for this shit. I most definitely didn't have time to babysit a twenty-two-year-old female with a doll's face and a bombshell's body.

Fuck.

As Arlo slowed the car, Harper leaned forward, her attention on the scenery outside the window. I didn't follow her gaze. I knew what she saw—a dark, thick forest with trees so tall they appeared to scrape the sky. The moon peeked from between clouds heavy with rain, revealing little of the narrow private road that cut through the woods.

We rounded a bend, and Draithmere appeared, its chimneys as tall and dark as the trees that surrounded it. Four stories of weathered brick, the house sat on a rise with the Olympic Mountains as a backdrop.

Harper's eyes widened, her blue irises ringed by a darker navy color. The scant moonlight caught in her hair, which spilled over one shoulder. It was neither blond nor red, but something in between. *Strawberry blond.* Wasn't that what people called it? It was a fanciful color. Feminine, like her. She looked nothing like her father.

No, she'd inherited her looks from her mother. According to the information Arlo found, Margaret Ward died of early-onset dementia just before Orson's scandals broke. The medical bills for her care had put the family finances on shaky ground. A series of bad investments on Orson's part made everything worse. His professional misconduct was the final straw. To raise funds, he'd sold the newspaper the Ward Family founded over a century prior. The family home was protected by a trust set up by Harper's mother, but the rest of the money was gone, and the house was in such a deep state of disrepair it would cost tens of thousands of dollars to restore it.

Harper had learned of her father's fall from grace during her first semester in journalism school. Arlo's research cleared her of any wrongdoing. She didn't deserve to pay for her father's crimes. Sharing his name would almost certainly make it difficult for her to work in her chosen profession. A good man wouldn't have used her as a bargaining chip with her father. A decent man would have put her on a plane to Chicago and wished her the best finishing her degree.

Unfortunately for Harper Ward, I was neither good nor decent.

The car jolted, and static electricity rushed through the cabin.

Harper yelped as she jerked in her seat. She glanced around the car, her shoulders tightening. "What was that?"

"The second of three magical boundaries that circle the

property. They increase in intensity, so you probably didn't notice the first one. The third will hurt."

"Hurt?" She hugged her midsection. "How? And what do you mean by *magical boundaries*?"

"Exactly what it sounds like. They're defensive spells designed to keep out unwanted guests."

Skepticism shimmered in her eyes. "Spells," she said flatly.

"That's right."

"So you're a witch as well as a lycan?" She tilted her head. "Or is it wizard?"

I pulled out my flask. The damn thing was nearly empty. "I sense sarcasm, Miss Ward. It's almost as if you don't believe I'm a lycan." I downed the last of the witch's brew and tucked the flask in my pocket. Harper tracked every movement, her jaw set in a way that let me know she'd clenched her teeth.

She seemed to realize she'd wrapped her arms around herself, and she moved her hands to the edge of the seat on either side of her slim, denim-clad thighs. "I like to think I have an open mind. But I admit it's difficult to believe."

A hum filled the air. Energy built, and magic pushed at me from all sides. Harper gasped. A second later, the car crossed the third boundary. Magic sizzled, then rained tiny sparks over my skin.

"Ow!" Harper jumped. Panic flitted through her eyes, but she covered it quickly. She couldn't control her heart rate, though. Her chest heaved as the rapid *boom, boom, boom* filled my ears.

"How about now?" I asked, letting a smile touch my lips.

Anger brimmed in her eyes. She opened her mouth like she meant to issue a sharp retort. Then she seemed to think better of it, and she snapped her jaw shut and stared out the window.

And, once again, I was *not* disappointed.

We reached the house a moment later. Arlo stopped the car

outside the long stone building that had once served as a stable but now functioned as a garage. He fetched Harper's sole suitcase from the trunk, and I led us through the low-lying fog that hovered above the path connecting the garage to the main house.

"I can carry my own bag," Harper said behind me. Arlo's response came in the mild voice he used any time someone made an absurd suggestion.

"I've got it, Miss Ward. Watch your step. The pavers are old, and some might be uneven."

The fog swirled more thickly as we approached the steps. Vanilla teased my nose, followed by hints of honeysuckle. I clenched my jaw. The trip was over. Now, it was time to get back to the business of running Draithmere—and put my unwilling house guest out of my head for good.

The house guest in question made no effort to hide her curiosity as she trailed me inside. Her head moved on a swivel as she took in Draithmere's large, two-story foyer with a grand staircase that split halfway up and led to separate wings. A large pedestal table dominated the center of the space, which was decorated in rich mahogany. Paintings hung here and there, depicting landscapes and bowls of fruit. Things I didn't care about but kept around because they filled the walls. The furniture was nice enough, I supposed. Old and solid, unlike the modern garbage that came in flat boxes and ended up in landfills a decade later. As we passed an antique curio cabinet, Harper slowed, peering more closely at the design painted on the front.

"No dawdling," I said. Her sharp intake of breath hit my ears, and her stare was a laser between my shoulder blades as I led her to my study. Arlo brought up the rear, his footfalls audible because he allowed them to be.

The fire leapt high in the hearth as we entered the study,

and Harper jumped in place, her startled gaze going to the flames.

"Sit," I said, pointing to one of the chairs in front of my desk as I strode to it and seated myself.

Her reddish brows pulled together. "I'm not a dog."

I looked at Arlo, who'd stopped just inside the door. He lowered Harper's suitcase to the ground and gave me an inquisitive look.

"Do you need something, Your Highness?"

"Yes. If Miss Ward doesn't sit her ass in the chair like I ordered within the next fifteen seconds, put her in it."

"Yes, sir."

Harper's eyes shot sparks as she crossed the study and perched on the edge of the chair like it was contaminated. She let her backpack slide to the floor. A second later, she nudged it into a different position with her foot.

Interesting.

I met her gaze over the desk. "I make all the rules at Draithmere, Miss Ward. And while you're here, you'll follow them. For your own safety."

Fear glimmered in her eyes, but she hid it well, that stubborn chin of hers lifting again. "Is that a threat?"

"Yes."

Her lips parted in obvious surprise. Clearly, she hadn't expected that answer.

"Now," I said, "hand over your phone."

She stiffened. "You're not taking my phone."

"It stopped working the moment you entered the car. So it's quite useless to you." As the pulse in her throat fluttered more quickly, I waved a hand. "Go ahead and check if you want. I'll wait."

She stared at me for a second. Then, slowly, she leaned to one side and pulled her phone from her back pocket. She ran her thumb over the screen. When the phone failed to light up, she pressed the button on the side. Then she gripped it in both hands and pressed all the buttons. She gazed at the darkened screen, a swift parade of disbelief, anger, and fear crossing her features. When she lifted her head at last, she'd settled on wariness.

"More tricks," she said.

"Energy drains are child's play when it comes to magic. All of my vehicles are spelled to wreak havoc on cell phone batteries. Draithmere is the same. I like my privacy, and I won't have the human authorities tracking my movements or sniffing around my property." I knew my smile was less than friendly. "The same goes for reporters."

She swallowed. "If the phone won't work, there's no reason for you to take it."

"As I told you before, I'm very thorough. Also, I don't trust you." I tapped the top of the desk. "Now give me the phone, and we can avoid any ugliness."

For a moment, she appeared ready to dig in her heels. Then she leaned forward and set the phone on the desk, not quite slamming it onto the wood. "Do I get phone calls while I'm in your prison?" she asked, bitterness lacing her tone. "Bread and water?"

I slid her phone into the top drawer of my desk. "Arlo is a proficient chef. He'll see to it you don't starve."

"How long will you keep me here?"

"We covered this in your father's office, but maybe you were too distracted to pay attention. You'll remain at Draithmere until I'm satisfied your father has upheld his end of the bargain." I looked past her to where Arlo stood at the ready. "Show Miss Ward to her room, please. I'm sure she's tired."

"Yes, Your Highness."

Harper gripped the arms of her chair. "I have a life. School.

I'm a semester and a half away from finishing my degree. You can't—"

"Good night, Miss Ward."

"What if you're never satisfied that my father turned everything over?" Her voice climbed, panic lacing her words. "You can't just keep me here forever."

Her cheeks were flushed. The pulse in her neck fluttered like the wings of a trapped bird. Her full breasts thrust against her sweater, which was much too thin for the fall weather. Dammit, she needed a coat. Her nipples were puckered under the wool. Her long, glossy waves streamed over her shoulders. The glow from the hearth turned her hair the color of fire.

I should have never taken her.

"Sir," Arlo said softly.

I jerked. He stood right next to me, his hand on my shoulder.

"What?" I snapped, my voice rough and deep. In my peripheral vision, Harper watched us with avid interest. My heart raced. Wood creaked, and I looked down to find I'd gripped the arm of my chair so tightly my knuckles were white.

Arlo gave my shoulder the slightest squeeze. His dark gaze was steady. "You should eat, Your Highness. And perhaps a drink is in order."

Harper's regard was a weight against the side of my face. Pressing. Seeking. Delving under my skin. The heat from Arlo's fingers sank through my shirt.

"Yes," I said. "A drink would be...good."

Arlo stepped back. "Of course, sir. I'll see to it at once." He rounded the desk, his gaze on Harper. "If you'll follow me, Miss Ward, I'll take you to your room." As he spoke the last word, the fire in the hearth roared so high, the flames licked at the mantel.

Harper jumped to her feet and spun toward the fireplace.

The fire continued to blast from the hearth as if a dragon hid behind the stone and vented its ire on the study. A whiff of brimstone floated on the air. The lycans carved into the stone around the mantel appeared to shift and writhe among the flames.

Harper stood rigidly, tension in every line of her body. Arlo waited next to her abandoned chair, his gaze on the flames and his hands clasped lightly behind his back. Slowly, Harper looked at him, her profile illuminated by the blaze.

Arlo offered her a polite smile. “Do you have any food allergies or dietary restrictions?”

She blinked. “No.”

“Very good.”

Harper stared at him for a beat. Then she turned her gaze to mine, her expression wary once more.

I rested my hands on the arms of my chair. “You have nothing to fear under my roof, Miss Ward. As long as you follow the rules.”

CHAPTER FIVE

HARPER

I stood in the center of my new prison with my arms wrapped around my midsection.

Admittedly, the room didn't look much like a prison. For one thing, it was actually two rooms: a bedroom and an attached sitting room.

"I hope you'll be comfortable," Arlo had said moments ago when he placed my suitcase on a low bench at the foot of the bed. He didn't mention the fire in the study—or Einar's strange, sudden rigidity behind the desk.

The bedroom was as beautiful as the rest of the house, with a huge four-poster bed, an upholstered chair with a matching ottoman, and a big, glossy chest of drawers with a large mirror on top. A fireplace opposite the foot of the bed was cold, its grate littered with dead leaves. As visions of the raging fire downstairs filled my mind, I turned my attention to the rest of the room.

The bed was crafted from dark wood, with an intricately carved headboard and plush-looking bedding. The oversized chair and ottoman were a soft cream with gold stitching. Side tables flanked the bed. The grand mirror above the chest of drawers boasted a gilded frame. If I had to guess, the gold leaf was the real deal.

The sitting room was just as luxurious, with an inviting-looking sofa, another big chair, and more Victorian furniture. I was by no means an expert, but my mother had loved the period, and I had an eye for distinguishing replicas from true antiques. Einar's house was like a well-kept time capsule.

Or the home of someone born a hundred and fifty years ago.

I shoved that thought aside as pressure in my bladder had me scanning for a bathroom. My gaze snagged on a slightly open door, and I crossed the room and then exhaled in relief as I stepped into a spacious en suite with a claw foot shower-tub combo and modern plumbing. I relieved myself, then washed my hands with lavender-scented soap and tried to ignore how the basic, everyday task amplified the extreme oddness of my predicament.

After I dried my hands, I examined my reflection in the mirror above the sink. My eyes were red-rimmed, my face pale. It had to be close to midnight. I was late taking my medication. I fetched my backpack from the bedroom, returned to the bathroom, and dug the orange prescription bottle from the bottom of my bag. Shaking a pill into my hand, I downed it with handfuls of water from the sink. Then I splashed more water on my face and blotted it dry. As I finished, a knock sounded from the bedroom. Arlo's muffled voice drifted after it.

"Miss Ward? I brought you something to eat."

A hunger strike probably wouldn't get me anywhere. Besides, I hadn't locked the door. And, anyway, something told me Arlo had the key for every door in the house. Suppressing a sigh, I went to the door and opened it.

Arlo stood on the threshold, a polite smile on his boyish

face and a large tray of covered dishes in his hands. "May I?" he asked, hefting the tray a little.

I stepped back. He breezed past me, then placed the tray on a table next to the chair.

"I hope you like roasted chicken," he said, straightening.

"As long as it's not poisoned." The minute the words left my mouth, I wanted to claw them back. Arlo seemed nice enough, but he worked for Einar. Anyone who went along with threats and kidnappings was dangerous by association.

He regarded me now, his expression as unflappable as ever. "If Prince Einar wanted you dead, you and I wouldn't be having this conversation."

I swallowed. "Is that supposed to be reassuring?"

"His Highness can be surly on occasion, but he's always fair. He's also a man of his word. Ah, that reminds me." Arlo reached behind him. A second later, he extended a sheaf of papers.

The contract from my father's office.

Except I'd just seen Arlo bend to set down the dinner tray —and the papers hadn't been in his pocket.

"It's a copy of the contract," he said. "Prince Einar wanted you to have it for your records."

My heart thumped hard against my ribs as I took the papers. "Thanks."

"Of course. Now, unless you need anything else, I'll leave you to your dinner before it gets cold. Don't worry about the tray when you're finished. I'll collect it in the morning." Arlo went to the door. Just before he opened it, he stopped and looked over his shoulder. "I strongly advise against leaving your room tonight. And it would be imprudent to venture outdoors. We're isolated here in the mountains. You don't want to run across any of the wildlife that roams the countryside." He smiled. "Fortunately, you have everything you need right here in your suite."

"Right," I said, my voice hoarse in the quiet room. I clutched the contract in tight fingers. Nerves tingled down my spine, memories of Einar's claw and the out-of-control fire parading through my head.

Arlo nodded. "Good night, Miss Ward." He left, closing the door gently behind him.

For a moment, I just stared. Then I rushed to the door, locked it, and stumbled back. *Oh, Dad, what have you gotten me into?*

Fresh anger kindled in my chest as I looked down at the contract. With a muttered curse, I went to the chair and flung the papers next to the tray of food. The copy of the contract was useless to me. As Einar had helpfully pointed out, I wasn't a party to it. Never mind that it was *beyond ridiculous* for him to act like putting a kidnapping and blackmail scheme in writing somehow made it legal.

But as bad as Einar was, my father was worse. He'd put me in danger to supposedly salvage a ruined career. Most people went through life never knowing what it would take for a loved one to sell them out. Now I knew exactly what my father thought of me. I was worth a couple of Pulitzers and a crumbling house.

Tears burned my throat. At the same moment, my stomach let out an angry growl. I wiped at my eyes, my gaze going to the tray. My airport bagel was a distant memory. Plus, I wasn't supposed to take my medication on an empty stomach. And Arlo had a point. If Einar wanted me dead, he could have accomplished it a dozen different ways between Seattle and Draithmere. Why go to all the trouble of hauling me to his house just to poison me?

I went to the table and lifted the largest cover. Golden-brown chicken, mashed potatoes and gravy, and plump rolls glazed with butter were arranged around a plate. Growing up, my mother's job had given me access to all sorts of professional kitchens, and I knew quality food when I saw it. Heavenly scents wafted from the plate, and my stomach released another insistent growl.

Before I could lose my nerve, I sat and began to eat. As Einar promised, Arlo was an excellent cook. The chicken was flavorful and well-seasoned. The rolls melted in my mouth. Arlo had included two beverage options: water and a glass of light brown liquid that turned out to be iced tea.

As I ate, my gaze returned again and again to the fireplace. The flames downstairs had roared like they were ready to break free of the hearth and engulf the whole room. Except something held them in check. Something...or someone.

No. That was too damn outrageous to believe.

In journalism school, I'd been taught to pursue the truth. To follow the facts wherever they led. If I let fear rule me, I risked missing something important. And I had to stay rational. What was more likely, Einar controlling fire with his mind, or Einar being some kind of wealthy weirdo who enjoyed scaring the shit out of people? Maybe he styled himself as a Bruce Wayne/Batman type with Arlo as his Alfred.

Except Arlo hadn't seemed like a butler when he rushed to Einar's side downstairs. He'd squeezed Einar's shoulder, and for a few tense moments, it had appeared as if the men's roles reversed, with Arlo in charge and Einar obeying commands. Einar had gone from ordering me to my room to staring me down like he wanted to jump the desk and rip my throat out. Firelight had flickered in his eyes, sheening the silver with a layer of gold.

Like the video.

Suddenly, the food I'd eaten settled like a rock in my stomach. I stood and went to one of the big windows in the sitting room. No bars covered the glass. I tested the latch, and the window opened like normal, allowing chilly night air to sweep into the room. A rustling, scratching sound at my back made me whip around, my heart pumping faster.

The dead leaves in the fireplace stirred, scraping the stone. Relief swept me, and I released a shaky breath as I faced the window once more. Outside, an elaborate hedge maze sprawled over grass splashed by moonlight. My breath puffed in white clouds as I braced my hands on the sill and leaned over it, trying to gauge the distance to the ground.

My heart sank. The bedroom had to be at least three stories up. There were no balconies. Not even a vine clinging to the brick. Unless I got brave—or desperate—and knotted bedsheets together, escaping through the window was out of the question.

Another gust of icy wind tugged at my hair as I looked over the maze. The hedges were taller than my head, and they seemed to extend forever. Far enough to get lost in.

A shiver raced down my spine.

I pulled my head back inside and shut the window. Fatigue tugged at me, and I let my shoulders slump as I faced the bedroom. *What a fucking day.* The hours of airport travel, the meeting with my father, and the long road trip with Einar pressed down on me like a weight.

But my stomach was full, and I was unharmed. The bedroom was nicer than any hotel I'd ever stayed in. And Einar was a mystery to unravel. If I had any hope of escaping Draithmere, I had to figure out its master. What motivated him? What were his weaknesses? If I followed the facts, I'd find the truth eventually.

But first, I needed sleep.

I went to my suitcase and pulled out pajama pants and a T-shirt. In the bathroom, I arranged my toiletries along the back of the sink, lining them up until they were even, the labels facing outward.

Except one bottle touched the one next to it.

I nudged the first bottle aside a little.

Then a little more.

There. Now they were even.

Tendrils of panic crept through me. Wait, were they *really* even? I crouched, eyeing the travel-size bottles of shampoo and face wash. After a moment of examination—and a few more nudges—the panic receded. Still crouching, I rested my forehead against the sink's cool porcelain. When the last of the anxiety faded, I stood, avoiding my reflection in the mirror.

I brushed my teeth and washed my face, then piled my hair in a messy bun and slathered night cream on my skin. Maybe I was a captive but, dammit, I was going to be a well-moisturized one.

Returning to the bedroom, I grabbed my notebook from the bottom of my suitcase. My heart squeezed as I flipped through the notebook's first few pages, where my mother's neat, careful handwriting marched down the lines. I knew every word by heart, which wasn't difficult since the handwriting only spanned a handful of pages. She'd recorded notes and recipes from her final interview. Here and there, the sentences trailed off. Even then, she'd struggled to remember things.

But she passed on her love of old-fashioned pen and paper to me. She always hated using a laptop on the job. *"It puts a barrier between you and the person you're interviewing. Writing by hand is so much more personal. It takes more effort, and it shows the person you're speaking with that they're worth your time."*

If only I'd had more time with her. But I had pieces of her life. I carried the notebook to bed and climbed in, sitting cross-legged against the pillows. Pen in hand, I flipped to a blank page in the back. When she died, I never intended to write in her notebook. How could I desecrate it that way? Then I imagined my mother laughing at me, her blue eyes crinkled in the corners.

Desecrate, Harper? Really?

Mom never took herself too seriously, even though she had every right to. I couldn't talk to her anymore. But I could reach her in other ways. I'd inherited her love of cooking—of tinkering in the kitchen and trying new things. I could make the recipes she'd collected over the years. And I could put my words in her notebook, carrying on the career she'd loved so much. All voices died eventually. But words were permanent. If you wrote something powerful enough, it could outlast you.

I balanced the notebook on my knee and began to write, describing my long day of travel. My anger and frustration at being forced to put my semester on hold. The bitterness of arguing with my father. My shock at seeing the photos and videos. When I got to Einar, I paused, visions of him pinning my father to the bookcase popping into my head. After a second, I started writing again.

He's tall. When I squint, he could almost be Chris Hemsworth.

Immediately, a different memory flooded my mind. I stood at my father's desk in the newspaper office, a school essay I'd written in my hand. My father took it, plucked a red pen from the holder on his desk, and marked up my paper while I tried not to fidget. A second later, he handed the essay back.

"You described your main character as Tom Holland. It's lazy writing to use a known person as a reference. Do the hard work and tell the reader what your character looks like."

Biting my lip, I crossed out "Chris Hemsworth" and substituted "dark blond hair" and "silver eyes." I filled in more detail, describing Einar's build and demeanor. His clothing and obvious wealth. The arrogance that set my teeth on edge. I stopped again. Then I drew a deep breath.

He claims he's a lycan prince.

I stared at the words. Outside, the wind picked up. A moment later, it howled down the fireplace and into the bedroom, sending a gust of cold air over the bed.

What if Einar wasn't just an eccentric rich guy with odd habits? What if he was exactly what he claimed to be? And if he was, where did that leave me?

I set the notebook aside, scrambled under the sheets, and yanked the comforter to my chin. A lamp on the bedside table filled the bedroom with a soft glow. Exhaustion swept me, and my eyelids grew heavy. Einar couldn't keep me shut in the bedroom forever. Problems always looked better in the morning.

I'd figure out my next steps then.

CHAPTER SIX

HARPER

I bolted upright in bed, a loud noise ringing in my ears. For a second, I swam in my muddled thoughts as I stared at a strange fireplace. Sunlight filled an unfamiliar room full of dark wood and elegant furniture.

All at once, recognition slammed into me. This was Einar's home. And I was his prisoner.

A high-pitched shriek sounded from the direction of the window, the sharp sound lifting the hair on my nape.

I tossed the blankets back and scrambled out of bed. Another scream split the air as I rushed to the window and yanked the curtains wide. On the grass below, a woman in a tattered white dress swayed on her feet at the entrance of the hedge maze.

The morning sunlight painted her in stark colors, emphasizing her pale skin and long black hair. Her dress clung to a painfully thin body, holes in the fabric showing her skin underneath. She paced, her bare feet sinking into the grass, which was covered with a layer of frost that sparkled like diamonds in the sun.

It was too cold for her to be barefoot, let alone wearing a dress that looked ready to fall apart.

She flung her head back and gave another broken cry. Even from a distance, I could see tears running down her cheeks and the tendons of her neck stretching taut.

Had Einar locked her up, too? Whoever she was, she clearly needed help. I reached for my phone, but of course I didn't have it.

The woman continued wailing, her mouth stretched wide and her hair falling around her shoulders in a wild tangle.

I whirled from the window and flew to the door. Fumbling with the lock, I yanked the door open and fled down the hallway, my bare feet pounding against the soft carpet runner. The hallway looked different in the light of day, but I managed to retrace my steps from the night before, and I raced down the grand staircase as quickly as I dared. When I reached the foyer, I hesitated, my ears pricked for the woman's cries. Sunlight streamed through stained glass windows and cast colorful patterns on the hardwood floors.

A mournful cry drifted from behind me. I spun and then followed it, rushing down a short hallway lined with closed doors. A second later, I burst into a spacious, modern kitchen. I got an impression of stainless steel appliances and gleaming marble countertops before another shriek sounded from outside. A pair of wide French doors opened onto an expansive patio. The hedge maze lay behind it.

And the woman stood at the maze's entrance, her back to me as she screamed into the sky.

I hurried to the doors, wrenched them open, and rushed down a set of concrete steps. Chilly morning air sliced through my T-shirt as I crossed the patio, ran down another set of steps, and onto the grass. The frost stung my bare feet. Dew soaked the bottoms of my pajama pants, but I barely registered the discomfort as I jogged toward the woman. Up close, her dress was even more tattered than I'd thought. The hem was ragged, its edges stained brown as if the dress had once been long enough to drag on the ground.

"Are you okay?" I called.

The woman stiffened. I stumbled to a halt as she faced me.

Her tears were gone, her eyes clear. With no more than twenty feet between us, it was easy to see she was stunningly beautiful, with deep blue eyes and pouty red lips.

And her dress was intact, the white fabric pristine and perfectly tailored. The hedges rose behind her, the bright green a lush backdrop to her dazzling beauty.

Even as I grappled with the sudden change in her appearance, an image flickered over her like an old-fashioned film strip skipping. One second, she was normal. The next, she held her severed head in one hand and a shallow silver bowl in the other. The eyes in her severed head blinked slowly. Her hair trailed to the frozen ground.

I staggered backward, my heart in my throat and a gasp on my lips.

The woman tipped the bowl. Blood spilled over the edge and splashed onto the grass.

I cried out, terror gripping me.

The woman jumped as if I'd startled her, and the horrible vision vanished. Now, she appeared as she had from the beginning, her head firmly on her shoulders and her gown in ruins. Tears ran down her face. Terror filled her eyes. She drew a deep breath and gave an ear-splitting shriek.

I clapped my hands over my ears, cringing as pressure built against my eardrums.

The woman snapped her mouth shut. Between one breath and the next, she transformed into a crow and soared over the hedge maze.

"No!" a man's voice shouted. I spun as Einar thundered down the patio steps, his arms pumping. "Myrna, no!"

The crow flapped its wings hard, climbing into the air and streaking over the maze. It swooped once before flying out of sight.

I stood with my arms limp at my sides, my mind reeling from the spectacle I just witnessed.

Einar sprinted across the grass and staggered to a stop, his chest heaving. His face was stricken as he stared at the spot where the crow had disappeared. He wore nothing but a pair of black sweatpants slung low on his hips. A mat of dark blond hair covered his chest before narrowing to a thin trail that ran down rippling abs before disappearing into his waistband.

I jerked my gaze from his hips just as he rounded on me with a furious expression.

"Are you pleased with yourself?" he demanded.

I jolted. Why did he seem angry with *me*? But he wasn't surprised—which meant this wasn't the first time the woman had done this. And it wasn't a video I could dismiss. She'd changed right in front of me.

"She transformed into a bird," I said, still trying to wrap my mind around it.

Einar scowled. "Because you frightened her!"

Was he serious? Outrage made me take a step toward him. "You're blaming this on me? Her *head* came off! She screamed like she was dying."

"No shit. She's a banshee." He looked toward the sky, and he spoke under his breath as if he talked to himself more than me. "Now, she'll take forever to coax back to the house, assuming I can find her."

"Banshee," I repeated, my nerves still jangling. "Like the Irish spirits who scream when someone is about to die?"

Einar looked at me, irritation in his gaze. "Not spirits.

Humans always get it wrong when it comes to supernaturals." He stalked to me, grabbed my elbow, and hustled me toward the house. "Come on. You have no business being out here."

"Hey!" I dug in my heels, but it was useless. He was simply too strong, and I was forced to stumble along even as I tried to twist from his grip. "What do you mean, you have to coax her back to the estate?"

He ignored my attempts to break free, and he kept his gaze straight ahead as we neared the patio steps. "I don't have time for a reporter's questions."

"Then you shouldn't have imprisoned one in your house!" His strides were so much longer than mine, I had to practically run to keep up with him. As we started up the steps, I stumbled, banging my big toe against the concrete. "Ow! Motherfucker!"

Einar stopped, and he relaxed his grip on my elbow as I bent and clutched at my foot. Pain shot up my injured toe, and I hissed in a breath.

"Shit!"

"You have quite the potty mouth, Miss Ward," Einar said.

I glared up at him. "If you don't like it, let me go, and you'll never have to hear it again."

He gave me a mild look. "What makes you think I don't like it?" Without warning, he bent and swept me into his arms. I gasped in surprise, clutching at his broad shoulders to steady myself. His bare chest brushed my arm where my T-shirt sleeve had ridden up.

"What are you doing?" I asked, trying to sound more indignant than flustered.

"You're hurt," he said as he carried me up the rest of the stairs and into the house. "I don't have time for injured reporters, either."

Now, my indignation threatened to choke me. "I wouldn't

have gotten hurt if you hadn't dragged me across your backyard!"

He grunted as he strode down the hallway, carrying me like I weighed nothing. "Stay inside like you're supposed to, and things like this won't happen."

Oh, he was an asshole. I clamped my mouth shut, holding my body rigid in his arms. His chest was warm against my shoulder.

No. He was *hot*, almost as if he ran a fever. But he didn't look sick.

Because he's not human. The thought landed like an arrow thunking into my brain.

Everything Einar had told me was true. Having just witnessed a woman transforming into a bird and flying away, I couldn't deny reality anymore. Einar was everything I'd seen in the video in my father's office.

A lycan.

A prince.

Over a century and a half old.

I swallowed the whimper that tried to rise in my throat. My father's actions were even worse than I'd thought. He'd known exactly what Einar was, and he'd signed me over to him anyway.

Einar didn't even break a sweat as he ascended the stairs and carried me down the hall. He shouldered into my bedroom and deposited me on the rumpled bed.

"Stay there and don't move," he said, stepping back. Before I could protest, he left the room.

I stared after him for a second, indecision warring within me. Did I get up and make a run for it? But where would I go? It wasn't like I could sneak downstairs and steal a car.

At least not just yet. Not in broad daylight, with Einar and probably Arlo ready to catch me.

Filing that plan away for later, I leaned forward and examined my toe. The skin was bloodied, but the injury was little more than a scratch. The pain had dwindled to a dull ache.

Einar returned with a white metal box in his hands. Immediately, the room felt smaller.

"Don't touch the wound," he said. "Your hands are dirty."

I bristled. "My hands are fine."

The bed dipped as he sat on the edge. He flipped the box open, revealing an impressive first aid kit.

"I don't need any of that," I said, drawing my knees to my chest. With mild horror, I realized my feet were dirty from running barefoot outside. But at least my toenails were painted. I couldn't afford professional pedicures anymore, but I did the best I could. Not that I cared what Einar thought.

He snagged my ankle and pulled my leg straight, and he huffed as he shoved the leg of my pajama pants to my knee. "Which is why you're bleeding on the sheets. Don't move, or I'll tie your ankle to the bedpost."

Heat rushed into my cheeks. "You can try."

He ignored me as he ripped open a small, square packet. The astringent scent of alcohol seared my nostrils. Einar held my foot steady and swiped the pad over my toe, cleaning the blood and dirt. For a second, everything was cold and wet. Then the scrape caught fire.

"That hurts!" I tried to pull my foot from his grip, but he latched onto my ankle again, his fingers so hot they were like a brand against my skin.

"It's better than an infection," he said, tossing the alcohol pad aside and grabbing a tube of ointment. I winced as he applied it to my wound. But after a second, the stinging faded, leaving only the faintest ache.

Einar blotted the injury with a pad of white gauze. When the wound stopped bleeding, he ripped open a long, stretchy kind of gauze, then pulled scissors from the kit and began trimming a bandage. He worked as if he treated injuries all the time, his movements quick and competent. After a minute, I forgot to fight as I watched him set the scissors aside and then wrap the gauze around my toe. He wound it around and around with the perfect amount of pressure—not too tight but not so loose that it risked falling off—before tying the ends and tucking them under one of the neat edges. Then he smoothed a hand up my calf as he lifted my foot and appeared to admire his work.

"It should heal in a day or two," he said. "You can get this wet, but no soaking in the tub. Just showers."

My throat went dry, and a strange heat spread through me as his fingers pressed into my muscle. My leg was bare from the knee down. And he was shirtless, his naked shoulders golden in the morning sunlight pouring through the windows. The beams turned his hair a lighter blond. More blond scruff covered his jaw. He braced a bare foot on the rug next to the bed. His other foot was tucked under him.

And his sweatpants had slipped lower when he carried me. They strained across his lap, where a bulge left no question that he was well-proportioned for a man his height.

The heat in my cheeks flared higher. "Thank you," I muttered, tugging my foot from his grip.

He let me go, and our gazes met...and held. His lashes were long for a man, the tips curling slightly upward. Like his hair, his silver eyes were lighter in the sun. He'd treated my injury. Yes, he caused it, but he made sure it was clean and properly tended.

The air shifted, a curious kind of tension filling the space between us. Einar's brows drew together. Then he blinked, and the spell was broken.

He stood, towering over me with suddenly angry eyes.

"Now you know what I am. So you understand why it's dangerous to wander the grounds. You won't do it again."

Any pleasant feelings I might have felt toward him vanished. "I was trying to help that woman."

"Well, you didn't. And she doesn't need your help."

"Who is she? Your wife?"

His eyes widened slightly, obvious surprise in the silver depths. "Myrna? No. I don't have a wife."

What about a girlfriend? I squashed the thought before it could form on my lips. The last thing I needed was him thinking I was interested. However, his relationship status would definitely tell me more about him. At the very least, it would open up new lines of questioning. Was he single? Did he pine for a lost love? Maybe he carried a torch for a female lycan who rejected him in his youth.

Einar grabbed the first aid kit and tucked it under his arm. The giant box seemed tiny against his large form.

"Is Myrna a relative?" I asked.

He gave me a look that let me know he was onto me. "She's a guest, just like you. And just like you, she does what she's told. So stay in your room." He went to the door.

I clambered from the bed and stood with my fists clenched. "I can't just sit in this room all day. I'll go crazy."

He turned from the door. "I thought you were writing a story about me. Isn't that what all your questions are for? Uncovering my secrets?" His expression hardened. "Here's some advice, Miss Ward. Stop digging. Because the more you find, the more reason I'll have to keep you here indefinitely."

He left, slamming the door behind him.

CHAPTER SEVEN
EINAR

I left Harper and went straight to my study. The fire burned low, its heat doing battle with the chill that drifted from the windows.

I rooted in my desk drawers, clenching my jaw as each one failed to yield a flask.

"Dammit," I muttered, bending and rifling through the deep bottom drawers I rarely opened. Fire seared my veins, anger pumping hotter with every beat of my heart.

My fingers closed around something hard.

A flask.

Fucking finally. I fell into my chair, my hand shaking as I unscrewed the top and tipped my head back.

The flask was empty. I shook it, and a few drops of witch's brew landed on my tongue. Not nearly enough. The fire in my veins climbed higher. Sweat beaded on my skin.

Flinging the flask into the open drawer, I gripped the edge of the desk and raised my voice. "Arlo!"

"I'm here," he said, rushing into the study. Relief pounded through me at the sight of the flask in his hand. "Freshly brewed, sir," he added, coming to the desk and handing the flask over.

I yanked the top off and downed half the contents in a single gulp. As the witch's brew set fires under my skin, Arlo watched me with a concerned expression.

"It's been a while since you needed this many doses in such rapid succession."

It took a minute for the fire to dim sufficiently for me to speak. "I'm fine. Last night's brew was weak."

Arlo's horns flickered in and out of view. "I'll check the dosage."

"Good idea."

He glanced at the windows. "I thought I heard Myrna."

"You did," I said, swiping the back of my hand across my mouth. "Harper heard her, too. And saw her. They had an encounter."

Arlo's eyes widened. He lowered himself into one of the chairs in front of my desk. "Is Miss Ward all right?"

"Considering she saw Myrna shift and then take to the sky, I'd say she's doing pretty well." I relayed the whole story, explaining how I'd arrived too late to stop Myrna from flying off. As I spoke, Arlo's horns grew more solid, the black spirals curving against either side of his head. When I finished, he exhaled heavily.

"Myrna will return. She always does."

I screwed the top back on the flask. "Leave some nuts and dried corn near the maze's entrance. She'll probably stay in beast form. Flying makes her hungry. The food will attract her."

Arlo nodded. Then he looked at the flask on the desk, his dark eyes thoughtful. His horns faded, only to reappear a second later.

"What is it?"

He hesitated.

"I pay you to be honest with me, Arlo. What's bothering you?"

"Miss Ward is nothing like her father."

I grunted. "She's a reporter. She's everything like her father."

A smile touched Arlo's lips. "She's definitely curious. But that's natural given the circumstances, don't you think? Draithmere isn't an ordinary house. Now that she's seen Myrna, she's bound to have questions."

"Trust me, she has no problem asking them." Unbidden, images of Harper standing in the morning sunlight flashed in my mind. Her T-shirt had clung to her chest, leaving little to the imagination. Her nipples had pushed against the paper-thin material like little spears. In the sun, her hair looked more red than blond. And when I lifted her in my arms, the scent of vanilla and honeysuckle had clouded my lungs. It wasn't her perfume. It was *her.*

The fire crackled, jerking me from my thoughts. Arlo watched me, and I realized I'd lapsed into silence.

"Um..." I cleared my throat. "Anyway, that...happened."

Arlo was quiet for a moment. And he seemed to choose his next words carefully. "Miss Ward has a kind heart. And she's been through a great deal these past few years."

I sat back in my chair. Had Harper charmed Arlo in the short time they'd interacted? An uncomfortable sensation stirred in my chest. I rubbed at my sternum. *Probably heartburn.* I pinned Arlo with a look. "You disapprove of the way I've handled her."

"It will be difficult to keep her in her room all the time. If she discovers—"

"She won't," I said. "I assume you told her to stay away from the maze?"

Arlo sat taller in his chair, a hint of challenge in his eyes. "In my experience, Your Highness, the fastest way to tempt someone into exploring a forbidden area is to tell them they can't go near it. Miss Ward trained as an investigative journalist. I can only assume that warning her away from the maze will end with her sneaking outside to get a better look at it."

Damn. He was probably right. I rubbed at my mouth. "We'll have to find something else for her to do. Maybe put a television in her room."

Arlo frowned. "Do you think that will be enough to occupy her?"

"Give her your streaming passwords, then. Women like movies, right? Dramas. Romance shows."

Arlo's frown turned into something that might have been bemusement. "I'm not sure that's a universal rule."

Irritation flared. I drummed my fingers on the arm of my chair. "Fine. Order some books for her."

"I could..." he said slowly, appearing to consider it.

I stopped drumming. "But?"

"But you should be prepared for her to ask about her college coursework. Miss Ward doesn't strike me as the type of person to let that go."

"The university isn't going anywhere. She can finish her studies when my business with her father is concluded. Speaking of which, have you heard from our scheming friend?"

"Orson sent an email in the early hours of the morning. I was on my way in here to tell you when I heard you searching for a flask. Orson insists he turned everything over."

Yeah, right. I dug in the pocket of my sweatpants and withdrew the gauze I'd saved from treating Harper's toe. As I dropped the handful of bloodied material on the desk, Arlo's nostrils twitched.

"It's hers," I said. "Send it to Ward."

Arlo swallowed. "Should I send a note?"

"Just tell him it's from me. Let him wonder how I got it. I want him checking his mail, worried I'll send worse."

"Yes, sir." Arlo's horns grew more solid.

I let my gaze linger on them a moment before meeting Arlo's stare. "My tactics might seem harsh, old friend, but they're in our best interests. And Harper's. Don't you want her back at school, learning how to delve into people's private lives without shame or remorse?"

Arlo didn't rise to the bait. He simply took the gauze from the desk and stood. "I'll send this as you instructed, Your Highness."

I suppressed a sigh. "Thanks. And don't forget about the books and TV."

"Of course not, sir. Consider it done."

"Have there been any rumblings from the Puget Sound Pack?" A change in leadership was always a volatile time within a werewolf pack. Depending on how many wolves threw their hat in the ring, dozens of pack members could die in the dominance contests that followed. Which was perfect.

"Nothing," Arlo said. "It appears they're licking their wounds."

"We cut the head off the snake. If they pick a new alpha, we'll repeat the process until the pack is too depleted to survive." Like any social group, packs needed numbers and a hierarchy. The Puget Sound Pack was small, but it had been well-organized under Rex Addington. He'd been dominant enough to compel the respect and obedience of even the most vicious wolves. From what I knew of the pack, no other wolf was strong enough to keep the rest in line. The remaining wolves were likely to drift to other packs. Some of the stronger ones might attempt to live as lone wolves. If they did, I'd pick them off one by one.

"I'll keep my ears open for any developments," Arlo said.

"Thank you."

He left, and I slid lower in my chair, my gaze on the fire. Maybe Arlo was right to disapprove of me sending the blood-stained gauze to Ward. But I couldn't keep Harper in my house. If it hadn't been clear to me before, it was now. She was a nuisance. A...distraction. The sooner she left, the better. In the meantime, I had to keep my distance.

No matter what happened, I was staying as far away from Harper Ward as possible.

CHAPTER EIGHT

HARPER

And then the woman shot into the air and transformed into a crow.

I stared at the words I'd just written. Biting my lip, I scratched out "woman" and wrote "Myrna." Banshee or not, she had a name. According to Einar, she wasn't a spirit.

But was he a reliable source? It wasn't like I could ask him. I hadn't caught so much as a glimpse of him in three days. On the other hand, I'd seen plenty of Arlo.

Every time I opened my door, the steward appeared. The first day, he'd rounded the corner just as I stepped from the bedroom. The second day, he was dusting the banister as I approached the stairs.

And this morning, he met me in the hallway with a breakfast tray in his hands.

"No need to come downstairs, Miss Ward," he said cheerfully. "I'm happy to bring your meals to your room. I'm sure you'll be more comfortable eating in there."

It was as if Arlo possessed an uncanny ability to know when I left my room. After witnessing Myrna's terrifying decapitation and inexplicable transformation, I could only assume he did. He looked human, but that didn't mean anything. The memory of him pulling the copy of Einar's contract from thin air still hovered in my mind.

I tapped my pen against my lips as I snuggled more deeply in the oversized chair next to my bed. My gaze strayed to my bare toes peeking from under the throw I'd draped across my lap. The scrape from the patio steps was fully healed. Apparently, Einar wasn't worried about me developing sepsis. He hadn't even inquired about the injury through Arlo.

Whatever. Einar's silence was a *good* thing. He was cocky and overbearing. He'd kidnapped me, and now he had Arlo serving as my warden. I didn't want to hear from him.

But his absence meant my reporting had hit a dead end. Pursuing Myrna's story was a pivot. And, if I was honest with myself, a way to keep from losing my mind. The problem was I knew next to nothing about banshees. Maybe if I asked Arlo for some books on Irish folklore...

I let my gaze drift to the sitting room, where stacks of books lined the low table in front of the sofa. Moonlight glowed through the windows, casting the sitting room in shades of silver.

Arlo had delivered the books—along with a flat screen television—the same afternoon I saw Myrna transform. "I can order more books," he'd said with a shy smile. "Just give me a list of the genres you like to read."

I'd folded my arms. "Did Einar tell you to bring these? Nice of him to make my cage more comfortable."

Arlo's smile faded. "Prince Einar isn't a monster."

I raised a brow. "He transforms into a wolf under the full moon."

"Oh no, Miss Ward, that's a myth. The moon has no effect on lycans. Or werewolves, for that matter."

"What about silver?" I asked, my fingers itching for my notebook.

"Another myth."

"Garlic? Or is that just for vampires? *Are* there vampires?"

Arlo seemed to consider his answer. Finally, he offered a soft smile. "There are more things in heaven and earth, Miss Ward, than are dreamt of in your philosophy." He went to the door. Before he left, he turned back. "Prince Einar told me you visited the maze. It's best to keep your distance. The hedges can be disorienting if you venture too far inside."

A shiver sprinted down my spine. "Will I encounter a ghost as Hamlet did?"

Arlo opened the door. "Good night, Miss Ward." He slipped from the room, leaving me alone once more—and no closer to gaining my freedom. His unspoken order was clear: I could watch television, and I could read. But I couldn't leave my room.

And under no circumstances could I go anywhere near the hedge maze.

Cold air whistled down the hearth, pulling me from my memories. Setting my notebook aside, I stood and went to one of the windows in the sitting room. As I had every night for the past three nights, I stared down at the hedge maze, which gleamed in the moonlight. It didn't *look* disorienting. The turns and angles were straightforward enough.

What was Einar hiding? Arlo's warning to stay away tripped senses I'd honed since I was a child in my family's newspaper office. It wasn't anything I could articulate—just a "wrongness" that compelled me to stop and take a second look. But investigating was impossible as long as I was unofficially confined to my room.

Frustration rose, and I squinted, trying to peer into the center of the maze. Dammit, the next time I saw Arlo, I was going to ask him what was so dangerous about a bunch of manicured shrubbery. Let him go on the record denying the maze held any significance. Then I could prove him wrong.

A knock rang out.

I turned from the window, braced to hear Arlo call through the door as he usually did. On the other hand, it was too late in the evening for food. Maybe he could read my thoughts, and he knew I was prepared to call him on his bullshit. Or maybe something was wrong.

Dad. My father had been so volatile since my mother died.

I rush to the door and yanked it open. "Is everything oka—?" I snapped my mouth shut at the sight of the creature in front of me. No taller than my hip, he stared up at me with green eyes that glowed like gemstones. A shock of white hair waved back from his face, which was humanoid but covered with an intricate tattoo the same shade as his eyes. His ears tapered to points, and a pair of stubby black horns protruded from his forehead. His tight black T-shirt showed off muscular arms, and his jeans were artfully ripped at the knees. More green tattoos swirled down his forearms. A chain ran from one of his belt loops to his pocket.

I jerked my gaze down the hallway, expecting to see Arlo barreling around the corner.

"He's off tonight," the creature said in a deep, scratchy voice at odds with his size. He flashed an apologetic look before sweeping an elegant bow. A tail curled around his hip, the end tipped with a tuft of white hair. "I didn't mean to startle you, Miss Ward. I'm Goliath."

I blinked. "Um..."

He straightened, his eyes twinkling. "I'm aware of the irony."

I couldn't help my smile. "I'm happy to meet you, Goliath."

He brightened. "Really? I was worried I'd frighten you.

Everyone said I shouldn't come to your room, but they changed their minds when I pointed out how Myrna made a bad impression. We don't want you thinking we're all like that, screaming at strangers and then flying off without so much as a hello."

It took me a moment to absorb his words. "Everyone?" I asked.

He nodded. "My friends in the maze. They're all curious about you. Prince Einar has never brought a human home before."

Goliath made me sound like a stray dog, which probably served me right for thinking of him as a "creature." But I got the sense he wasn't trying to insult me.

"Does Einar often bring people to Draithmere?" I asked.

"Not all that often. Maybe a few times a year. Sometimes their families call. Other times, he finds them."

I really needed my notebook. "And the people he finds... They're like you?"

Goliath smiled, showing the tips of small white fangs. "There aren't many like me around. But we have all kinds of supernaturals in the maze." He tilted his head, and his tail waved back and forth as if he was excited. "I could introduce you if you want. Everyone wants to meet you." His tail curled around his hip. "Prince Einar called you a reporter when you spoke near the maze. Do you write for a newspaper?"

Old pain tried to surface, but I pushed it away. "Not now. But I used to. Well, sort of. My family owned a paper while I was growing up. My father sold it a few years ago." God, I was rambling. I drew a deep breath. "I'm close to getting a bachelor's degree in journalism. Maybe I'll write for a paper once I graduate."

Goliath appeared to take all this in. "So, would you like to visit the maze?" His expression turned mischievous. "Arlo doesn't take a night off very often. This could be your only chance."

Indecision gripped me. Goliath didn't seem like a threat. On the other hand, I'd just met him—and he was most definitely not human. Arlo's warning ran through my mind. *The hedges can be disorienting if you venture too far inside.*

What if Goliath intended to lead me into a trap?

"I'm sorry," I said. "Maybe another time."

Goliath's eyes dimmed, but he recovered quickly. "Of course, Miss Ward. I understand." He jerked a thumb over his shoulder. "I should get back. I need to tell the others so they can take everything down." He backed up. "Well, good night."

Guilt twinged in my chest. "Good night."

He turned and started down the hallway. His tail drooped behind him, the white tuft at the end brushing the floor. It was like a miniature lion's tail. But the rest of him was utterly unique. And he'd been so polite.

"Wait!" I called.

He stopped and turned back. "Yes?"

I stepped into the hallway. "Why do you need to tell the others I'm not coming? What are they taking down?"

"Oh. Well..." Pink spots appeared on his cheeks. "We planned a little welcome party. Like I said, most of the supernaturals in the maze have never met a human. They were excited to talk to you." The pink deepened. "We've seen you watching the maze from your window at night. They thought you might like to interview them. A lot of us are lonely, since we're separated from our families."

Oh my, they'd planned a party for me? And they *wanted* to answer questions? I could find out what lay inside the maze—and possibly learn more about Einar. Which could lead to getting out of Draithmere and going home.

"Can I bring my notebook?" I asked.

Happiness glimmered in Goliath's eyes. "Of course."

I nodded. "I'll be right back. And then I'd love to visit the maze with you."

~

TEN MINUTES LATER, NERVES CRAWLED OVER MY SKIN AS I TRAILED Goliath across the lawn. With every step, I waited to hear Einar bellowing for me to stop.

Goliath met my gaze over his shoulder. My anxiety must have showed on my face, because he flashed a reassuring smile. "You don't have to worry about Prince Einar. I cloaked us."

"What does that mean?"

"It's part of my magic. It doesn't really hide anything, just makes people far less likely to look in my direction. As long as you stay close to me, it'll cover you too."

I moved closer, but we were already at the maze's entrance.

Goliath held out his hand. "This only works if you enter with one of us."

My heart knocked against my ribs. I'd tucked my mother's notebook under an old corduroy jacket that buttoned down the front. The notebook's spiral binding dug into my skin, but I welcomed the pressure. It reminded me I was alive. My mother had missed out on so many things. I had the opportunity to explore a world that wasn't supposed to exist. It was the ultimate scoop. I had to go get it.

I took Goliath's hand. "All right. I'm ready."

His gemstone eyes reflected the moonlight. "It's as easy as stepping forward. Okay? One, two, three."

We entered the maze.

And the world changed in a blink.

The hedges were gone, replaced with soaring pine trees.

Goliath and I stood on a forest trail lined with wildflowers in a riot of colors. The sky was the purple of twilight. Stars winked among fluffy white clouds. Mountains rose in the distance, their peaks capped by snow that looked like a giant had placed a dollop of frosting on every peak.

A warm breeze tugged at my hair, bringing the scent of pine and flower blossoms to my nose. Somewhere nearby, an owl hooted. When I turned toward the sound, I spied a waterfall spilling down the side of a mountain like a glossy blue ribbon.

"It's beautiful," I breathed, stepping toward it. The second my foot left the trail, water misted my face. I blinked, and the waterfall was directly in front of me, its roar drowning out my startled cry.

A tug on my hand jerked me backward. I stumbled, then gasped as Goliath steadied me. When I swung my head back toward the waterfall, it appeared in the distance once more.

My heart pounded as I turned back to Goliath. "How...?"

"Time and space work a bit differently here," he said. "The Fae built the maze for Prince Einar." He lowered his voice to a conspiratorial whisper. "They do good work, but sometimes you just want a door to be a door, know what I mean?"

I wiped water from my face with a shaking hand. "Yeah."

"Don't worry, Miss Ward. Just stick to the trail, and we'll get to the party without any trouble."

"Please, call me Harper." I smiled. "All my friends do."

Goliath beamed at me, his tail waving. "Harper it is."

We continued down the path, the beauty of the maze all around us. Fireflies danced among the trees on either side of the trail, their glow guiding our way. After a moment, the sound of lively music drifted toward us. A few more steps, and the trail veered right and then opened onto a clearing.

I caught my breath. A party was in full swing. It was a

small gathering, but the participants were clearly enjoying themselves. A tall, dark-haired man played a fiddle as a woman and another man danced. Colorful lanterns hung from the trees above the clearing. Soft moss carpeted the ground. A huge tree stump appeared to serve as a table, its surface cluttered with teacups and a large platter piled with cakes and pastries. Smaller stumps around the clearing held candles that glowed as brightly as the lanterns. A black cauldron hung suspended over a fire, its contents bubbling. The cauldron looked like something straight out of a Halloween store display.

The woman whooped, her long skirts swinging in an arc as her partner spun her around. The woman was lovely, with stunning features and a willowy figure. But her hair, which flowed to her waist, was the same color as the moss under her feet.

Her partner's hair was just as boldly colored. Fiery red, it cascaded down his back in a riot of curls. A matching beard shadowed his jaw, and his white teeth gleamed between his lips as he smiled. At first glance, he looked like an ordinary human with really great hair. A closer look revealed amethyst eyes that glittered in the moonlight.

They were a gorgeous couple, and they moved with a gracefulness that was impossible not to watch.

Between one twirl and the next, the man's hair burst into flames.

I jumped, a yelp bursting from me.

The musician stopped playing. The couple stopped dancing, and the woman propped her hands on her hips.

"Not again, Leander!" she cried, her chest heaving.

The man's hair continued to blaze, the plume of fire leaping for the sky. But his face and body remained untouched, and his expression was more annoyed than panicked as he strode to the table, picked up a pitcher of water, and dumped it over his head.

The flames went out, revealing the man's charred, hairless skull. I pressed a hand over my mouth as my stomach threatened to revolt. The man wiped water from his eyes, then shook his head like a dog emerging from a swimming pool. Brilliant red hair sprouted from his head and fell down his back, the locks as glossy as if the fire never happened.

"Show off," Goliath murmured beside me. When I turned to him, he'd folded his arms, and his expression was affectionate as he watched the man. "Phoenixes and their hair."

As Goliath said the last, a faint *pop* split the air.

Everyone in the clearing focused on us.

"I beg your pardon," the redheaded man said. "It's *plumage*." He approached us, a smile spreading on his face. Up close, his hair was threaded with long, red feathers that appeared to spring directly from his scalp. He looked at Goliath. "And you've been a naughty dragon, hiding yourself and our guest on the sidelines." He plucked my hand from Goliath's and bent over my fingers. "Enchanté, Miss Ward. I'm Leander."

"Hello," I said, my heart pumping faster. Wait. Was Goliath a *dragon*? I couldn't help but gape at him.

Goliath gave me a mild look. "Never judge a book by its cover."

"I..."

"Oh, leave her alone," the woman said, crossing the clearing. She shouldered Leander out of the way. "And stop flirting, you rake." She smiled at me as she extended a hand. "Adina Norwood, bog witch."

I shook her hand. "I'm Harper Ward. Um, human."

Adina turned and cupped her hands around her mouth. "It's all right, Keir! Leander stopped bleeding."

The man with the fiddle nodded. A second later, he winked out of sight. Another second, and he appeared next to Adina.

"I'm Keir Holland, my lady," he said in a clipped English accent. Prominent fangs flashed as he spoke. "It's an absolute delight to meet you."

As I opened my mouth to respond, an enormous brown bear lumbered from the pine trees. I sucked in a breath, but Goliath put a hand on my arm.

"It's all right. It's just Rolfe. He always forgets to shift when he's tired." He raised his voice. "Hey, Rolfe! Go put some clothes on!"

The bear stopped. It blinked slowly, then looked down at its front paws. With an irritated-sounding groan, it turned and disappeared into the woods.

Goliath looked at me. "He'll be back in a second. Fingers crossed, he'll be wearing pants."

"Should we have tea?" Adina asked, gesturing to the tree stump table.

Leander offered me his arm. "This way, Miss Ward. You can sit next to me."

I placed my fingers on his elbow. "It's just Harper."

Five minutes later, I sat at the tree stump with a cup of tea at my elbow and a plate loaded with tiny cakes in front of me. Goliath and the others ate their cakes while Adina flitted around the table, pouring tea from a kettle she'd pulled from the fire.

A giant of a man in a pair of denim overalls trundled from the trees, yawning as he came to the table. Leander stood and shoved two chairs together.

"There you go, big guy."

The man sat heavily. Immediately, his head drooped, and he released a loud snore. As he tilted forward, Keir snatched a teacup from his path. Just as quickly, Leander caught the man's shoulders, then lowered the man's upper body gently to the stump.

The man sighed, a contented look spreading over his face as he continued snoring.

Leander gave the giant's head an affectionate pat. "It's okay, Rolfe." He met my gaze and dropped his voice to a stage whisper. "He's always like this when he's hibernating."

"He's a bear shifter?" I asked, unbuttoning my coat and pulling out my notebook.

"That's right," Leander said. "One of a handful left on the West Coast." Leander frowned as he slipped into his own chair. "Actually, Rolfe might be the only bear shifter left on this side of the country."

"Why?" I asked, flipping my notebook open. I wrote as fast as I could, scribbling down everything I'd experienced since entering the maze. "Did something happen?"

"War," Adina said, placing a tumbler with a straw and a lid in front of Keir. She smiled when he murmured his thanks. Then she sat next to Leander and turned serious eyes to me. "A century ago, there were five major bear clans. Then they started fighting. Skirmishes became battles. Battles turned into full scale warfare. The clans tried to wipe each other out. And they almost succeeded. Just two clans remain, and their numbers are dangerously low. The whole race verges on extinction."

I paused writing, and I looked at the top of Rolfe's head, where chocolate curls gleamed in the candlelight. "So Rolfe lives in the maze to escape the war?"

"He's the son of his clan's alpha," Keir said. "But Rolfe is unskilled in battle, and he takes too long to shift. He wouldn't survive long out in the world. His family would probably kill him before the rival clan could. So Prince Einar invited him to stay at Draithmere, where he can live in the maze."

My gut clenched. "His own family would kill him?"

Beside me, Goliath nodded. "Bears are very single-minded. Honor in battle is everything. Most bears believe that life without victory isn't a life worth living. Rolfe is different, but that doesn't make him any less of a bear. Not to us."

Leander thumped his fist on the stump. "That's right." The others murmured their agreement.

I looked around the table. "And the rest of you?" I asked. "Why do you live in the maze?"

Goliath gave me a level look. "My situation is similar to Rolfe's. I've never been able to shift into my beast form. Among my people, that kind of failure is unforgivable. Without the maze and Prince Einar, I would be hunted and killed."

I touched his hand. "I'm so sorry, Goliath."

"Don't be." He smiled around the table, the green tattoos on his face catching the light. "I have friends here."

A comfortable silence descended. The twilight had deepened, and the fireflies continued to bob among the trees that surrounded the clearing.

Keir cleared his throat. "I also came to the maze out of necessity. I'm a vampire, turned four centuries ago this week, actually."

"Ah!" Leander exclaimed, his smile bright in his beard. "Happy birthday. You don't look a day over three hundred."

"Thank you," Keir said, giving Leander a regal nod. "I try to take care of myself."

Hiding a smile, I bent my head and continued writing.

Keir waited until I paused, then offered a rueful expression. "As you might expect, I survive on blood. Unfortunately, I faint every time I see it." He tapped the side of his tumbler. "My friends are kind enough to donate and then place their blood in closed containers. But it hasn't always been that way. Europe during the Industrial Revolution was a tough place to live for a vampire who can't stand the sight of blood."

I rested my elbows on the table. "So what did you do?"

"Kept to myself as much as possible." Keir ducked his head. "And spent a lot of time passed out and nearly being incinerated by the sun." He looked up. "When telegraph lines first started stretching across England, I got word of a lycan prince who offered protection to supernaturals with...unique challenges. I wired Prince Einar, and he invited me to visit Draithmere. I've been here ever since."

An odd feeling spread through my chest. If Keir and the others were telling the truth, Draithmere wasn't a prison. It was a haven for supernaturals. And Einar wasn't a jailer. He was more of a...hero.

"I also came from Europe," Leander said. "I can't control my fire, so traditional employment options are out of the question. My kind are always trying to land jobs with wizards or philosophers. But I've always liked doing hair. I have a salon here in the maze."

Adina sat back in her chair. "I'm here because it's the only way I can stay out of prison."

Leander reached over and patted her hand. "The coven was jealous of your skills, Adina love." He looked at me. "Bog witches are the best potion masters in the world. Their products are highly sought after. But like any business, they're protective when it comes to their brand."

"They lack imagination," Adina said, her tone sour. "I've always liked experimenting. Corporate started sending threatening letters when I was in my teens. They didn't want me trying out new ingredients. But how are we supposed to stay competitive if we never branch out?"

"Are there other types of witches?" I asked. "Rivals who make potions?"

"Oh, yes." She counted off on her fingers. "Night crones, garden hags, the Baba Yagas. For a while, the harridans were really giving us a run for our money. Not that the general public can really tell the difference. Our products are basically the same."

"Like Coke and Pepsi," Leander told me.

"But the bog witches have had an edge for centuries," Adina said. "However, that doesn't mean you stop innovating."

I rested the end of my pen on my notebook. "So, you were innovating? And management didn't like it?"

"Exactly. I mean, there were a few mishaps in Florida, but—"

"What kind of mishaps?"

Adina waved a hand. "Just some potion work gone a little haywire. It's not like those men were trapped in manatee form forever."

Leander nodded as he looked at her. "That's right. And no one can blame you for the forest fire. It could have just as easily been that gender reveal party." He turned to me. "She was framed."

"It was corporate greed," Adina corrected. "Headquarters got nervous about me drawing too much attention to their stagnant operations. So they brought me up on charges and tried to throw me in prison. I came to Draithmere, where Prince Einar offered me a place to stay."

"And we're all glad he did," Leander said.

"Hear, hear," Keir chimed in, lifting his tumbler. I joined the others in raising my teacup to Adina, who blushed and waved off the toast. When we lowered our cups, Leander gave me an inquisitive look.

"What about you, Harper? Why did you come to Draithmere?"

"Oh." I fiddled with one of the cakes on my plate. "Well."

My face heated. Something told me they wouldn't look kindly on my father threatening to expose Einar and, by extension, the entire supernatural world. Would they hate me if I told the truth?

"You don't have to tell us," Goliath said.

"No, it's okay," I said, racking my brain for the simplest explanation. "My father and Einar had a disagreement. Einar is holding me at Draithmere until my father does what Einar wants."

Keir frowned. "That's not very chivalrous of Prince Einar."

"Lycans are an arrogant breed," Leander said, sighing. "But I trust that His Highness will do the right thing."

Rolfe jerked, rattling the cups on the table. He released a snort that echoed around the clearing, then lifted his head and blinked big, brown eyes. "What did I miss?"

For a moment, everyone stared. Then laughter broke out. Adina pushed a plate of cakes toward Rolfe.

"Eat," she said. "We'll fill you in."

The party continued, conversation and tea flowing. Keir stood and begin playing a slow, sweet melody on his fiddle. Leander pulled Adina to her feet and swept her into a waltz. The sky slid from purple to midnight blue, the stars winking like diamonds. More fireflies dipped and fluttered among the trees. A few times, a pair of glowing eyes gleamed from between the pines.

"Just curious passersby," Goliath assured me. "A lot of folks in the maze are shy. Like Myrna."

"What's her story? Will she ever return to the maze?"

"Oh, yes, don't worry about that." Goliath lowered his voice. "Her situation is a lot like Leander's in that she can't control her power. So she ends up terrifying innocent people on accident. It's all very embarrassing for her, which is why she flies off to the mountains when it happens. But she always returns. Well, either that or Prince Einar coaxes her back."

It was hard to imagine Einar having the patience for such a thing. I gazed around the clearing. "Why did Einar build this place? What does he get out of it?"

Goliath frowned. An aura of discomfort surrounded him. "I don't think he was looking to get anything out of it."

Oh no. I'd offended Goliath. Einar was a kidnapper, but Goliath clearly didn't think of him that way. I wouldn't get any of the answers I was looking for by insulting a man Goliath considered a friend.

"I phrased that poorly," I said. "I guess I just wondered why a lycan prince would go to such great lengths to build a sanctuary for other magical beings."

Goliath's expression grew thoughtful. "In the supernatural world, power is everything. Those of us with flawed magic usually don't live very long. Broken magic is dangerous and volatile. Difficult to control. I can't argue with the reality that it's safer for everyone when broken magic is buried and erased. To do that, however, you have to bury the one who wields it. I suppose Prince Einar thinks that price is simply too high to pay." Goliath turned his gaze to Leander twirling Adina around the perimeter of the clearing. "Or, to put it more simply, he believes we're worth more than our flaws."

I followed his gaze, doubts swirling as I watched Leander and Adina. Was I wrong about Einar? A pair of bright green eyes appeared on the edge of the forest. My heart sped up, and I leaned closer to Goliath. "Is anyone in the maze unfriendly?"

Goliath shook his head. "We're all here because we can't be anywhere else. We live peacefully. Draithmere is the only place where most of us can live at all. Many in the maze are antisocial because they come from traumatic backgrounds." He chuckled as another set of eyes appeared next to the first. "But that doesn't stop them from being nosy."

Adina came by and refilled my tea. A second later, Leander pulled her into another dance. They twirled around the clearing as Rolfe ate the rest of the cakes.

Eventually, I turned to Goliath. "I should probably go back."

He nodded. After a round of hugs and promises to return, I followed Goliath from the clearing and down the forest trail. Hand in hand, we stepped from the maze and onto the lawn. Wintry air seared my lungs. The moon was high in the sky, which was darker and less star-studded than the sky in the maze.

"It's different," Goliath said, clearly deciphering my thoughts. "Faerie is a more vibrant place than the human world. The Fae always make things warmer and brighter." He led me through the house, which was as quiet as we'd left it. When we reached the top of the grand staircase, I gasped.

"I left my jacket in the maze."

Goliath's brows drew together. "I can get it for you."

"No, it's okay." I tucked my notebook under my arm. "It's not a big deal."

Mischief danced in his eyes. "Now you have a reason to come back."

I laughed—and I got the distinct impression he was much younger than he seemed. "I promise I'll visit again. The party was lovely, and so was the company. Thank you for introducing me to your friends."

Goliath's tail appeared around his hip, the fuzzy white tuft like a dab of cotton candy. "The next time you visit, I'll show you the mountains."

"I'd like that."

"Later, Harper." He backed up, waved, then disappeared in a puff of black smoke.

I clutched my chest, my heart pounding. Good grief, what other powers did he possess? Shaking my head, I made my way to my room, memories of the party and the supernaturals I'd met making a smile tug at my lips.

The second I opened my door, my smile fled. Because my bathroom door was wide open, and a shadow splashed against the wall. Just as I gathered breath to scream, Einar burst from the bathroom with my medication in his hand.

My fear vanished. "What are you doing with that?" I stormed forward, swiping for the bottle. As I grabbed at it, my mother's notebook slipped from under my arm. It fell to the floor and flopped open. Lines of my handwriting filled the page.

Einar and I looked at it. Then we looked at each other. We went for the notebook at the same time, but he moved in a blur, snatching it from the floor.

"That's mine!" I cried, flying forward.

He lifted the notebook out of my reach, and he ignored me as I jumped, trying to claw it from his hands.

"My name is in here," he said, angling his body away as he studied the notebook. "Arrogance that sets my teeth on edge," he read. "Silver eyes and broad shoulders."

Oh my fucking god. Anger and worry warred within me. What if he read my notes from the maze? For some reason, it seemed important that he didn't find out I'd met Goliath and the others. "Give it back!" I demanded. "You have no right to look at my things!"

He met my gaze. "I do when you sneak out of your room." He stepped toward me, menace hovering around him. "Where were you just now, Miss Ward? And before you answer, know that my sense of smell is much better than yours. I can smell deceit, so it would be very foolish to lie to me."

CHAPTER NINE

EINAR

Harper darted looks at the notebook, her hands curled into fists at her sides. For a second, I thought she might actually take a swing at me.

"Give me the notebook," she said finally.

"Answer my question, and I'll consider it. Where the hell were you?"

The dusting of freckles on her nose was more prominent than usual against her flushed skin. "Fine. I was exploring the house."

I let her words roll over me. Scenting lies was rarely straightforward. Most people didn't speak in absolutes. Speech was the byproduct of thought, and thoughts were messy. But people also got nervous when they lied. Their heart rates picked up. They began to sweat.

I waited for Harper's perspiration to drift to me. Instead, vanilla and honeysuckle curled into my lungs. Like a switch being flicked on, arousal pumped straight to my dick.

The sudden rush of need had me speaking through clenched teeth. "So you were snooping."

Harper gave a furious-sounding gasp. "Like you have any room to talk!" Anger snapped in her eyes. "You can't expect me to stay in my room all the time. I'm a grown woman."

She certainly was, even though she was damn young. But she'd lived on her own for a long time. Arlo's report had been thorough, covering how Orson checked out when Harper's mother fell ill, leaving Harper to fend for herself. She'd navigated college alone, financing her studies with a small trust Margaret left behind. Which made me wonder if Harper's mother had known Orson couldn't handle money.

"Besides," Harper said now, "you never told me I couldn't leave my room."

"An oversight. I'm telling you now."

She clenched her jaw. Her hair was down, the strawberry blond strands streaming over her shoulders. She looked like an avenging angel who wanted to spill my guts onto the area rug. Which shouldn't have been hot but damn if it wasn't confusing the hell out of my dick.

With an angry sound, she grabbed for the notebook.

I jerked from her reach, then held the notebook aloft. Ignoring her frustrated growl, I scanned the page, where my name appeared over and over. What else had she written about me?

"That's private," Harper said.

"Chris Hemsworth?" I looked at her, interest tugging at me. "You think I look like him?"

"Absolutely not. That's why I crossed it out."

I thumped my knuckle against the page. "It says it right here, along with *broad shoulders*. Your descriptions are rather colorful. Are you writing a romance novel?"

"No." A look of disgust crossed her features. "I'm a journalist. I have no interest in writing romance."

I let a slow smile curve my lips. "Is that so? Sounds awfully elitist, don't you think?"

Her nostrils flared as she clearly recognized I'd flung her earlier words back at her.

"Well, either way," I said, "I'm flattered you used me for inspiration."

She held out her hand. "Give me the notebook, Your Royal Highness." She said the honorific the way someone might say *dickface*.

Deliberately, I flipped pages, skipping to the front of the book. But the handwriting changed. Now, recipes lined the pages. Here and there, notes explained an ingredient or clarified the directions.

Harper made a pained noise. When I looked at her, she'd gone pale.

"These are recipes," I said. "Whose handwriting is this?"

She swallowed hard. "My mother's. That was the last notebook she used for work before she died."

Silence fell. My chest tightened, and a powerful emotion swept me. It took me a minute to recognize it for what it was.

Shame.

I cleared my throat. "Arlo told me she was a well-known food critic."

"Yes," Harper said. She paused, as if debating whether to say more. "We used to cook together when I was young. Then she got sick..." Harper glanced at the notebook. "I planned to make all the recipes she left behind, but I got busy with school."

The shame intensified. I closed the notebook and held it out. Harper snatched it from my hand and held it against her chest like a shield.

"And my prescription?" she asked. "Am I allowed to have that too?"

I looked down at the bottle I'd forgotten I held. "I smelled chemicals," I said, handing it over.

She grabbed it and stuffed it in her jeans pocket, the round bottle snug against her hip. Something vulnerable huddled in her eyes, which were more violet than blue in the bedroom's soft light.

"Arlo has the night off," I said. "I realized you didn't get any dinner, so I came to ask what you wanted to eat. I knocked."

Harper stayed silent, her expression stony even as hurt swam in her eyes.

"You didn't answer the door. I wanted to make sure you were all right, so I came inside. When I didn't find you in the sitting room, I checked the bathroom." I nodded toward the white bottle cap poking from her pocket. "Like I told you, my sense of smell is much better than a human's. I scented chemicals. I wanted to make sure you're not hurting yourself."

Anger sparked in her eyes. "I'm not hurting myself. I'm helping myself. There's no shame in taking medication."

"That's not what I meant. Man-made medicines smell different than remedies that come from the earth." I hesitated, something cautioning me against calling the chemicals "unnatural." I gestured to the bottle again. "Do you need more of it? Are you sick?" Dammit, Arlo should have known if she had some kind of medical condition. I would have never brought her to Draithmere. I would have found another way to deal with Orson.

"I'm not sick," she said. She rubbed her lips together, clearly trying to decide whether to elaborate. Finally, she sighed. "I have an anxiety disorder. Medication keeps it from taking over my life."

I'd heard of such things. Worries that grew out of control. Goodness knew she had reasons enough to worry.

And I'd given her more.

But I'd also read that conditions like hers didn't necessarily require a reason. In some people, worries manifested for seemingly no reason at all. The anxiety could become constant and debilitating. It pitted the sufferer against a monster they couldn't see.

I met her gaze. "You're right. There's no shame in taking medicine. An ailment in the mind is the same as an ailment in the body. Treating anxiety is no different than setting a broken bone. You'll receive no judgment from me."

Her shoulders relaxed. "Thanks," she said softly.

I gestured to the pills. "This medication... It helps you?"

"Yes." She hesitated. "And talking to a therapist. But some behaviors still break through." She gnawed at her bottom lip, her teeth white and even—and fucking alluring as they pressed into the plump pink skin. "I line things up. Toiletries, bottles in the fridge, boxes in the pantry. I don't know why. Things just have to be in line. And I like it when the labels face outward. I hate that I do it, but I worry something bad will happen if I don't."

"Like what?"

"I don't know." She shook her head, her cheeks touched with pink. "I mean, logically, I know that straightening my shampoo bottle isn't going to change my life." She shrugged. "I guess if something had to be wrong with me, I'm lucky it's this. Other people have it a lot worse."

"There's nothing wrong with you." How could she think that? She was beautiful and smart. "Arlo says you're top of your class at Northwestern."

She huffed. "I was, past tense. Now that you've pulled me out of my classes, who knows what will happen to my GPA."

"You can finish your studies when my business with your father is finished."

"Right. I forgot about your ingenious and totally fair plan

to ruin my life because you think my father is hoarding video footage."

Ah, there was the Harper I was used to. The one who challenged me, with her stubborn chin and sharp words. Their reemergence shouldn't have made anticipation unfurl in my chest, something within me spoiling for another round of sparring. They shouldn't have made desire flare hot under my skin. I had no business feeling either of those things. Not with her. Not with anyone.

"What do you want for dinner?" I asked, hearing the gruffness in my voice.

She stiffened at the change in subject. And she flipped just as quickly as I had, any trace of softness fleeing from her voice. "I'm not hungry."

For a moment, I allowed myself to feel regret. I'd ruined our conversation—and the possibility of a more amicable relationship. But it was for the best. Harper Ward and I could never be friends. Or anything else.

"Don't be stubborn," I said. "You have to eat something."

She frowned. "I said I'm not hungry."

My temper rose. "So you'll punish me by starving yourself?"

Her lips parted on a gasp. "I know you're a prince, but did it ever occur to you that not everything is about you?"

I clenched my jaw. She might deny it, but she *was* being stubborn, and she *was* trying to punish me. For all I knew, her medication required her to eat.

"You're being foolish," I said.

She stepped toward me, her eyes shooting sparks. "First, I'm stubborn. Now, I'm stupid. Do you have any other insults to lob at me?"

"I said foolish."

"It's the same thing."

"Not really," I said. "Aren't you supposed to be a journalist?" I looked toward the sitting room. "I'll have Arlo bring you a thesaurus."

She pointed at the door. "Get out."

A growl rose in my throat. "No one orders me around in my own house."

A humorless smile touched her blue eyes, and her tone went saccharine. "New experiences can be hard, especially for someone your age."

My fingers itched to put her over my knee and swat some respect into her far-too-tempting backside. I bit the thought back before I could voice it and make everything worse. "You might not want food now, but what if you get hungry in the night?"

"Under normal, non-kidnapping circumstances, I'd go to the kitchen and get a snack. But you've made it clear that's not an option. So I guess I'll have to survive until the morning, Prince Einar. But don't worry. You don't need to concern yourself."

It was a clear dismissal. She'd called me *prince*, but she carried herself like a queen. She held my stare, defiance in every line of her body.

An exquisite body. She was irresistible in dark jeans and another tight sweater. How many of the damn things had she brought with her? They were a menace. The heat in my veins sizzled into something else. Something so very, very dangerous.

"Fine," I bit out, striding to the door before the fire could get too hot. "I won't burden you with my concern." I left, shutting the door behind me. And I shoved Harper from my thoughts as I stalked to my study with fire snaking through my limbs like lava.

Arlo had left an almost comical number of flasks in my

desk drawers. I sat and uncorked one, draining it in three gulps. As the witch's brew chased the fire, I bent my head and held back a scream.

Pain. It was forever useful as a distraction. It was also a faithful reminder of the consequences of letting myself think life could ever be different. Just one path lay open to me. I'd tread it for nearly a century. Straying from it was unthinkable. Too much depended on me staying the course.

Slowly, the burn faded. When I could lift my head without agony, I straightened. Whispers drifted from one of my bottom desk drawers. In the corner of my eye, the drawer emitted a faint glow. Ignoring it, I pulled a stack of papers toward me.

True to his word, Arlo had kept an eye on the Puget Sound Pack, and he'd left his findings for me to review. The news wasn't good. As I read, my mood went from bad to worse. The Puget Sound wolves had chosen one of Rex Addington's lieutenants as their replacement alpha—and the new boss was the same as the old boss.

In other words, a monumental asshole. But he was also a serious threat. I scanned Arlo's intel even though I was familiar with the new alpha and his background. Armand Reverdin had been kicked out of his pack in France for savaging a human in a public park. Werewolves were almost universally violent, but they avoided drawing the attention of the human authorities. Most alphas understood that secrecy was the best-case scenario for supernaturals. Humanity had a long and bloody history of targeting and killing anyone deemed "other."

I sat back in my chair, my gaze on the report. Reverdin was a conundrum. By all accounts, he was dangerous and volatile. Yet he'd served under Rex for close to ten years without attempting to challenge him. Now, the Frenchman had ascended to power.

The question was, what did he intend to do with it? I had

to find out. I needed to know what made Armand Reverdin tick. What his secrets were, and how far he'd go to keep them.

I turned my gaze to the window, where the maze gleamed in the moonlight. My own secrets drifted in the air like ghosts. I already knew how far I'd go to protect the people who depended on me. Their identities had to stay hidden. For many, discretion was a matter of life and death.

But the problem was even bigger than that. If the humans found out what I was, it was only a matter of time before they discovered the rest of the supernatural world. The result would be apocalyptic. Maybe literally.

Those were the stakes. Orson Ward had no idea what kind of chaos and danger he threatened to unleash.

It would be easier to kill him.

The thought had drifted through my head plenty of times. It was what my brother would have done. Cyrus acted swiftly and mercilessly when it came to protecting our race.

I knew that better than anyone.

But I couldn't kill Orson. Not now. Not after seeing Harper with that notebook. I wouldn't take another parent away from her.

Deep in my chest, the fire reignited. As I opened my bottom drawer to withdraw a second flask, the Book of Crubeus glowed like a beacon. Its cover was a lighter red this time. At the edge of my vision, flowering vines spread down the leather.

Honeysuckle.

I grimaced as I reached into the drawer, bypassing the book and grabbing the flask. "Not very subtle, are you?" I murmured, avoiding looking at the book directly.

Whispers floated from the pages, the words just a touch too quiet to make out. For a moment, curiosity tugged hard. Maybe tonight would be the night all my reading paid off...

No. The fire burned too hot for reading.

I slammed the drawer shut. The moment the book was out of sight, the whispers fell silent. As I uncorked the flask and drank, Arlo's voice rose in my memory.

"It's been a while since you needed this many doses in such rapid succession."

I tipped the flask back, letting the brew sear my throat. Arlo was wrong. The batches were weak, that was all. I'd have to speak to Adina.

But it could wait until tomorrow. Once Arlo returned, he could deal with Harper. He could deliver her meals and collect her laundry. He could find her new books to read. He could order her medication if she needed a refill. He could see to her needs. Someone had to.

It just couldn't be me.

CHAPTER TEN

HARPER

I picked at my lunch and tried not to think about lycan princes who commissioned magical mazes for supernaturals in need of a safe place to live.

The chair next to my bed wasn't the most comfortable spot to eat. For one thing, I had to balance my plate on the upholstered arm and then hope I didn't spill food down my shirt. Also, I'd spent so much time in the chair I was beginning to worry I might become one with it.

Maybe for dinner, I'd try the sitting room sofa. Chewing, I eyed the low coffee table through the opening that connected the two rooms in my suite.

No, it wouldn't work. I'd have to hunch over too far. The chair was better.

I sighed and went back to pushing my food around my plate.

My eyes itched from the sleepless night I'd endured after Einar left. So what if he saved Goliath and the others from discrimination and death? Einar's good deeds didn't change the fact that he'd bullied my father. His generosity didn't erase the bad things he'd done to me. Leander, Keir, and Adina were lovely, but maybe they never saw the side of Einar that was perfectly okay uprooting a human from her life and locking her in a bedroom far from home.

Maybe that was it. Einar didn't consider me an equal. The lycan lifespan was five hundred years. He'd made sure to point out his *superior* sense of smell. He could transform into a powerful and dangerous animal. Undoubtedly, he had other magical gifts.

By contrast, I was a twenty-two-year-old undergrad. Everything I owned in the world fit into a few packing boxes. For someone like Einar, I was merely a commodity—something he could maneuver around like a chess piece until he got his way. And when he finally got what he wanted, he would discard me and move on with his very long life.

The food Arlo had delivered suddenly tasted like ash in my mouth. I put my fork down and placed my plate on the table next to the chair. In a half hour, Arlo would come fetch it. Probably, he would bring a new book or two. He'd ask if I needed anything else and if I had any special requests for dinner. Then he would leave, and I'd be alone again.

And tomorrow, the pattern would repeat. How long before my sanity started to unravel?

I stood, a strange energy thrumming through me. I'd felt it from the moment I opened my eyes after finally falling into a fitful doze in the early hours of the morning. I was jittery and restless, like I couldn't escape my own skin. Despite the chilly wind gusting down the chimney, I'd been warm since I woke. My face was flushed, and sweat gathered at my temples. The next time Arlo showed up, I had to ask if he could adjust the temperature in the room.

On impulse, I pulled my sweater over my head, leaving me in nothing but yoga pants and a thin camisole with spaghetti straps. Stuck in my bedroom, I'd forgone a bra. I finger combed my hair back from my face and lifted it off my neck. Cool air teased my nape.

Whatever was wrong with me, it didn't bode well for—

A loud, sharp screech sounded from outside. *Myrna?* I rushed to the window and looked down. The sight in front of the maze was so outlandish, I almost rubbed my eyes like a cartoon character.

Two horses—one black and one Palomino gold—*battled* on the lawn. They grappled and pawed at each other, their hooves flying. The Palomino spun, its pale mane swinging, and kicked out with both back hooves. The black danced sideways to evade the blow. The Palomino kicked again, and this time it nailed the black horse in the ribs.

The black horse gave a high-pitched, angry-sounding neigh as it retreated. The Palomino pressed its advantage, galloping to the other horse and biting at its neck.

The black retaliated, head-butting the Palomino hard enough to send it crashing to the ground. It flailed on its side, tossing its head as it struggled. The black horse darted forward and ripped a chunk of flesh from the Palomino's flank. Blood spurted. The Palomino writhed in obvious agony, its eyes rolling. The black horse struck again, opening another nasty gash in the Palomino's side.

I moved without thinking, sprinting from the bedroom and hurrying downstairs. The foyer whipped past, and then I was through the kitchen and out the patio door.

The Palomino was on its feet. Blood streamed down its side, but it continued to fight, pawing and biting at the darker horse. They were massive animals, the muscles in their hindquarters bunching and flexing as they grappled. Foam flecked their mouths. Anger burned in their eyes.

Wait. That couldn't be right. They were horses. Animals

lashed out when they were frightened or in pain. They didn't fight to vent human emotions.

I hovered on the edge of the lawn, an eerie awareness lifting the hair on my nape. Without warning, the horses stopped attacking each other. As one, they swung their heads toward me. Their nostrils flared. The look in their eyes shifted from fury to...interest.

My throat went dry. Some deep, primitive instinct screamed at me to run.

"You little fool," Einar growled behind me. Before I could spin, a powerful arm gripped me around the waist and jerked me off my feet. Einar sprinted toward the house with me dangling from his arm like a ragdoll.

The horses charged, galloping after us.

A strangled scream caught in my throat. A second later, the world went sideways as Einar flipped me around and slung me over his shoulder. Pain exploded in my ribs. Einar didn't slow, just clamped an arm over the backs of my thighs and kept running.

The thunder of hooves filled my ears. Hair hung in my face, obscuring my vision. Sputtering, I flung enough hair out of my eyes to see the grass turn into the patio's concrete.

"Open the door!" Einar shouted, his voice sending vibrations through my chest. Seconds later, a zipping sound reached me, and then my body went weightless as Einar launched himself over the kitchen's threshold. He landed hard, and more pain stabbed at my ribs.

"Put me down!" I gasped, rearing up just in time to see Arlo slam the slider into place. On the other side, the horses reared.

Einar stopped, his shoulders heaving. He placed me on my feet, but I barely registered my newfound freedom. Because the horses were no longer horses. Not completely. Their bodies were still equine, but their torsos were human.

So were their faces. Two brutish-looking men stared through the window, their gazes locked on me. Intense emotion burned in their narrowed eyes. It was almost like... possession. My instincts fired again, urging me to flee the males who stared me down like they meant to hunt and claim me.

A shiver trembled through me. "Can they get in?" I asked hoarsely.

"No," Einar said, his shoulders heaving as he caught his breath. "The house is warded."

Relief loosened my knees, and I dared to break the horsemen's stares so I could focus on Einar. "Why are they looking at me like that?"

"They're centaurs. It's their breeding season. You tried to get between them during a dominance contest, and you smell like—" He snapped his jaw shut. He stared at me, tension rolling off him. The tendons in his neck stood out like he was holding himself in check.

"What?" I asked, my heart pumping faster. "What do I smell like?"

Arousal slammed into me, the juncture of my thighs throbbing so fiercely I doubled over. My vision blurred as moisture flooded my panties.

"Oh my god," I gasped, going to my knees on the kitchen floor. Outside, one of the centaurs roared. The sound vibrated the glass.

"Sir," Arlo said sharply. "You have to get Miss Ward upstairs. If this glass breaks—"

"I'm aware of the danger," Einar growled.

Another wave of arousal crashed through me. My nipples tightened, the tips throbbing in sync with the ache between my legs.

"I don't..." I croaked. "I don't understand." What the hell

was happening to me?

Another roar rattled the glass.

Arlo's footsteps rushed across the kitchen. "Prince Einar, you have to get Miss Ward out of sight!"

With a savage curse, Einar scooped me from the floor and rushed me from the kitchen. Another wave of need struck, and I cried out as I clung to his chest. The waves of arousal kept coming, each one climbing higher and crashing harder. More hot moisture dampened my panties.

"Fuck," Einar said, moving faster. He ran through the house and up the stairs, not slowing until he barreled into my bedroom and kicked the door shut behind us.

My body was a live wire, every nerve ending buzzing with an intensity that stole my breath. In some dim, rational corner of my mind, I knew something was very, very wrong. This wasn't normal, and I should most definitely be mortified. But I couldn't summon the will to care. Not with lust searing me from the inside out. As Einar deposited me in the center of the bed, I couldn't stifle my whimper.

Einar's gaze met mine, concern and frustration in his silver eyes. But there was something else too—an emotion I couldn't decipher. He braced a hand on the bed, his shoulders rigid. A delicious scent teased my nose. Pine, leather, and something indelibly masculine.

Him.

The ache between my legs pulsed harder. My panties were soaked, the fabric clinging to my most private places. I squirmed on the bed, a flush spreading down my chest. My heartbeat pounded in my clit, every beat accompanied by more moisture trickling from my pussy.

Einar sucked in a breath. Gold flickered over his eyes. And it should have been terrifying. Instead, it was *captivating*.

"What's happening to me?" I choked out, clutching at the

bedsheets as another wave of desire threatened to rip me apart. Sweat beaded my skin. My breasts throbbed, my nipples tingling. A glance down confirmed they thrust against my camisole like tiny arrow points.

For a moment, Einar just stared, a muscle in his jaw twitching as if he struggled to control himself. When he spoke at last, his voice was deeper than I'd ever heard it. "Centaurs are highly sexual creatures. Their lust must have affected you." He hesitated, the muscle twitching again. "Are you ovulating?"

"What?" I gasped.

"Something must have set them off. If you're fertile and... needy, they must have sensed it."

"I—" Another wave smacked into me, snatching my breath and tossing me into a turbulent sea of raw desire. My hips rolled of their own accord. The ache between my legs swelled to the point of pain. My vision blurred. I clung to the sheets, helpless to do anything but thrust my aching pussy into the air, desperate for friction. For anything. Fear rose along with my lust. The arousal was too much, the waves too high for me to endure.

"Help me," I gasped, tears burning my eyes. "Please, Einar, make it stop."

Einar's mouth tightened. He straightened, then stepped back.

"No! Please, don't go. Please. It hurts so bad." I was begging, but I didn't care. Nothing mattered but getting relief.

Einar rubbed a hand over his mouth. "Touch yourself," he muttered around his fingers.

I fumbled for my waistband, but my hands shook too badly. A cry of frustration broke from me as I failed to slide my yoga pants down my hips.

Cursing under his breath, Einar returned to the bed and brushed my hands away. He stripped the soft material down my legs and flung my yoga pants aside. After a moment's hesitation, he gave my panties the same treatment, leaving me nude except for the flimsy camisole.

Cool air hit my sodden pussy, the faint caress wrenching another cry from me as I spread my legs and reached for my clit.

"Fuck," Einar muttered, staggering back from the bed. The backs of his knees hit the edge of the chair, and he stumbled and caught himself. Gaze on me, he gripped the chair's arm and dragged the massive piece of furniture to the foot of the bed. He sat, his amber stare pinned between my thighs. Then he started giving orders.

"Use your juices," he rasped. "Slick yourself. Get your clit nice and wet."

I moaned as I complied, running my fingers down my folds and collecting the silky moisture before stroking back to my clit and rubbing in tight, fast circles. My thighs fell wide, and my hips rocked as my release hovered just out of reach.

"Harder," Einar said. "You're almost there."

Desire climbed, rushing me toward an apex. But just as I reached the summit, relief flitted away. "I can't come," I gasped, fear mounting.

"Yes, you can," Einar said, resting one hand on the top of his thigh. He curled his fingers into a fist, his knuckles instantly white. His eyes were a bright, eerie gold as he fixed his stare between my legs. I continued rubbing, my fingers almost too slick against my feverish flesh.

Einar growled long and low in his throat, the sound vibrating through me. "Use both hands. Open yourself."

My breathing grew ragged as I struggled to obey, my fingers slipping as I used my thumb and forefinger to part my labia. His stare was like a brand, his gaze burning from my clit to my opening, which gaped lewdly now that I held it open.

The scent of my arousal teased my nostrils, mixing with Einar's addictive essence. I dug my teeth into my bottom lip to keep from begging for him to pull the chair closer so I could drown in the leather and forest that clung to him.

"There you go," he growled, his deep voice yanking me from my runaway thoughts. "Spread your legs more. Knees flat on the bed. That's it. Now slide two fingers into your pussy. Go as deep as you can."

The barked rush of orders was like a lit match dropped onto the dry kindling of my desire. My back bowed, and my lips parted on a breathy moan. I obeyed, thrusting two fingers deep into my core.

"That's it," he said, approval thick in his voice. "All the way inside. Now fuck yourself with your fingers, Harper. In and out. All the way to the third knuckle. Don't stop until I say."

My face heated, but I didn't hesitate. Legs splayed wide, I pumped my fingers into my pussy, fucking my own hand. Thick, wet smacks lifted around the bed, the scandalous sounds mingling with my low whimpers.

Einar leaned forward, his elbows on his knees and his golden gaze locked on my sex. "Good girl. That is one soaking wet pussy, sweetheart. Your fingers are glistening. Keep fucking yourself."

My cries turned to moans. My hips bucked. But it wasn't enough. "Please," I rasped, finding Einar's gaze.

His eyes burned like twin suns as he held my stare. "Please, what?"

"Let me touch my clit. Please." Somehow, I knew I needed to ask. The game we played had unwritten rules, and that was one of them.

Einar stayed silent for a moment, his expression neutral as I continued plunging my fingers in and out of my opening. Then, in a voice like gravel, he asked, "Have you earned it?"

I moaned, my hips bucking harder. My orgasm was *right there*, my release within reach. It coiled inside me like a snake. "Yes," I said through clenched teeth, my whole body flushed and wanting. "Yes. I have to come. Please let me come."

Einar ran his eyes down my body, his otherworldly gaze taking in every trembling inch of skin between my neck and my toes. "Show me, then. Be a good girl and make yourself come."

With a wild cry, I moved my fingers to my clit. Two quick, furious circles and I was done, my orgasm breaking over me in a kaleidoscope of sensation and color. White-hot lust struck like a whip, lifting my hips from the mattress as I screamed my release. My vision dimmed, the world narrowing to the blurry pair of golden eyes observing me from the foot of the bed.

On and on my release went, delicious warmth sweeping me. One orgasm slid into the next. Through it all, the golden eyes never left me.

Eventually, the frenzy faded. Reality intruded, and I sprawled on my back, my body sheened with sweat and my heart thumping as I tried to catch my breath. Everything between my legs was swollen and hot. Little aftershocks rippled through me. The overwhelming lust was gone, my need satiated. Chilly air coasted over my body, raising goosebumps on my skin. My *bare* skin.

And Einar sat at the foot of the bed, observing everything like he'd bought a front-row ticket to a private show.

I scrambled upright, jerking the rumpled comforter over my lower half as I went. Embarrassment crashed through me like someone dumping a bucket of ice water over my head.

Einar stood, his eyebrows pulling together. "Are you okay?"

"I'm fine," I said, my voice hoarse from screaming the ceiling down. *Oh god, oh god, oh god.* Blood rushed in my ears as I tightened my grip on the comforter and clambered from the bed. I wrapped the heavy fabric around me like a toga and stood on shaky legs. My hair fell over my shoulders in a tangled mess—because I'd just *writhed* half-naked on the bed while Einar talked me through an orgasm.

He gave me an inscrutable look, his eyes silver once more. An aura of impatience huddled around him, as if he'd been roped into an unpleasant task and couldn't wait to finish. "The desire went away?" he asked.

"Yes. It's gone." I waited for a hole to open in the floor and swallow me. When it didn't, I tightened my grip on the comforter. "I'm sorry. I don't know what came over me. Whatever it was, I certainly didn't welcome it."

The temperature in the room plunged, filling the space between us with brittle currents. I glanced at the fireplace, but the dead leaves didn't stir. Weird. The draft must have come from the windows.

Einar's frown deepened. "The centaurs' magic is strong, especially when they're looking to mate. You shouldn't have been outside in the first place. I ordered you to stay in your room."

For a second, I was speechless. Then outrage rushed forth. "You're blaming *me* for what happened? Something I couldn't control?"

"You're responsible for your own actions. Unless you want me to believe someone forced you to open the door and run to the maze?"

My hand itched to slap the arrogant expression off his face. "I saw horses trying to kill each other."

"Centaurs, Miss Ward. How many times do I have to tell you that Draithmere isn't an ordinary house?"

"Are you serious? You don't tell me anything!" I bit back the urge to confess I knew all about the maze and the people within it. If Einar discovered I'd met Goliath and the others, he'd stop me from talking to them. And I'd lose my only opportunity to escape.

"I've told you what you need to know," Einar said. "I've kept it simple, Miss Ward. Until I'm satisfied your father has returned every shred of evidence he possesses about my true nature, you're my guest. And as long as you're here, you'll remain in your room. If you can't remember that single instruction, perhaps you should write it in your notebook."

Humiliation, hurt, and anger swirled in my chest, the noxious combination threatening to choke me. The notebook was more than paper and cardboard. More than a convenient place to write reminders. It was the only real connection I had to my mother.

"I want you to leave," I told Einar through clenched teeth. "And I hope I never see you again."

The chill in the air intensified. Einar's eyes seemed paler, the silver like chips of ice. "I'll have Arlo bring your dinner."

I didn't want it. But whatever. I forced myself to hold Einar's stare, my fingers aching as I gripped the comforter under my chin.

For a second, Einar seemed like he might say something else. But he just turned and walked out. Leaving me alone, my body as cold as the October air outside.

CHAPTER ELEVEN

EINAR

Harper's parting words ran on a loop in my head as I slammed into my suite.

"And I hope I never see you again."

Fine. It was better that way. But I didn't want it. At long last, I had to admit what I already knew. I didn't want to keep my distance from Harper Ward. No, I wanted to be in her bed. Inside her body. I wanted her strawberry blond hair wrapped around my fist while I put her on her hands and knees and thrust hard into her delectable cunt.

My jaw ached, and saliva filled my mouth as my fangs tried to descend. Pain throbbed deep in my bones, and a fire flared to life in the center of my chest. Gritting my teeth, I adjusted my straining erection as I stalked to my bedroom.

The bedside table was stocked with flasks. I pulled one out, wrenched the cap off, and poured the contents down my throat. Adina's brew went to work, scalding my veins like acid. Its fire was agony, but it chased the *other* fire away, which was all that mattered. When the flask was empty, I gripped the edge of the desk, squeezed my eyes shut, and rode out the burn.

Immediately, a vision of Harper appeared behind my lids.

She'd looked fucking perfect on that bed. Sweetly rounded hips. Firm tits concealed by the thinnest layer of cotton. Toned legs that went on forever. And between them, a plump, pink pussy with a pouty clit glossed with arousal. Her mound was crowned with a tiny patch of short, neat curls the same strawberry blond as her hair.

And damn if my mouth hadn't watered with the need to taste her there. To lick a path from those damp curls to her glistening cunt. She'd been so responsive, so eager to obey. To hunt down her pleasure and take it.

But none of that responsiveness had been for me.

No, she'd fallen under the centaurs' spell, her body caught up in magic-fueled lust no human could resist. She'd made that much clear the second she opened her eyes and remembered I was in the room. Then she'd scrambled from the bed and wrapped the comforter around her like she couldn't stand having my eyes on her.

"I don't know what came over me. Whatever it was, I certainly didn't welcome it."

Her words had landed like a punch to the gut. Which was precisely the reality check I needed. Harper Ward could never be mine. She had every reason to hate me. What else did I expect after I threatened her father and took her from her home? I'd uprooted her entire life, using her as collateral in a dispute that had nothing to do with her. Then I put her in a cage and told myself it was acceptable because I gave her a few books and access to television. I deserved every ounce of disgust she threw my way. The problem was, her disgust only made me want her more. Every flash of defiance in her blue eyes heightened my lust. Made me want to add more bars to her cage so I could keep her a little longer. It would piss her off. Make her hate me even more. And the perverse, twisted thing inside me that craved her would *like* it.

Blood pounded in my dick, my erection pressing painfully against my jeans. Sweat broke out across my body. A sharp *crack* split the air, and the edge of the desk gave way under my hand.

I stumbled backward, my eyes flying open. Blood dripped from my hand to the thick carpet. The bedroom rippled around me, the colors going neon bright before sliding back to normal. A huge splinter protruded from my palm. Although, *splinter* was too mild a word. The damn thing was like a two-by-four. Grimacing, I yanked it from my skin. More blood splattered the carpet even as the wound healed quickly.

"And I hope I never see you again."

"Whatever it was, I certainly didn't welcome it."

Biting back a curse, I lurched to the bathroom. After a moment's hesitation, I stripped and turned on the shower. I'd splurged the last time I redecorated, installing a walk-in with slate floors angled to let the water drain without issue. The showerhead was more complicated than the space station, and it was worth every penny. I set the water pressure on high, braced a hand against the wall, and used my other hand to work my dick.

I couldn't have Harper, but I had to get her out of my system. Only a man made of stone could have remained unaffected by her sweet scent and perfect pussy. In my mind, her fingers plunged between her glossy folds before stroking upward and circling her swollen clit. She'd gasped as I issued commands, a flush spreading over her peaches-and-cream skin.

Water pounded my nape. My balls drew up, my sack tight and aching. I worked my dick faster, the sound of Harper's arousal loud in my memory. She'd been completely uninhibited, her head thrown back and her tight nipples poking toward the ceiling as she fucked herself under my gaze.

Steam curled around me. My breaths grew harsh and uneven, involuntary grunts echoing off the shower's tile. I squeezed my cock, imagining myself plunging into Harper's warm, wet pussy. So hot and sweet. Like dipping my dick in liquid sugar.

I stroked harder, my fist tight around my pulsing cock. A guttural growl built in my throat. My heart pounded, each beat spurring me toward release. In my mind, Harper spread her legs wider, her pink folds dripping with honey.

The growl broke free, and I came hard against the shower wall, waves of pleasure washing over me. As I rode out my orgasm, images of Harper continued to flash through my mind. Her sleek body, the sensual roll of her hips, her soft cries of pleasure.

Shuddering, I pressed my forehead to the tile as I caught my breath. Blinking open bleary eyes, I watched the water carry my release to the drain. The whirlpool blurred as a wave of dizziness swamped me. Straightening, I fumbled for the tap. The world tilted, and I staggered sideways, thrusting a hand out just in time to keep from crashing into the wall and going down.

Fire flared in the center of my chest. Knives stabbed at my bones, the pain burrowing deep. The tiles blurred, coalescing into a grayish blob even as black huddled at the edges of my vision.

No. *Not now.*

The bathroom fixtures were hazy, indistinct shapes as I lurched from the shower and stumbled wet and dripping to the bedroom. A fierce ache lodged in my jaw as I pawed through the desk drawers and pulled out more flasks. I gulped one down...then another.

Black smeared my vision. A high-pitched ringing filled my head. This time, Adina's brew couldn't catch the fire.

"Arlo!" I shouted. At least I thought I did. I couldn't be certain with the blackness hovering and the fire scorching my bones to the marrow. Somewhere in my pain-addled brain, I realized I should have called for Arlo the moment I entered the suite. The fire had sapped my reason. I couldn't let the blaze overtake me in the bedroom. The location wasn't...secure.

A lightning bolt of pain struck the base of my spine. I doubled over, an unmanly whimper bursting from me. I sucked in a breath as color bled from the world. "Arlo!"

"I'm here," he said, his voice breathless. The smoke and sulfur stench of brimstone wafted around me as he gripped my shoulders and pulled me upright. His face was a fuzzy beige moon, but his sharp intake of breath told me I looked every bit as bad as I felt.

"Harper..." I croaked.

"I'll check on her later," he said. "Right now, we need to get you drinking." He dropped a hand from my shoulder and reached into the air.

"Too late," I said, my speech garbled as my fangs punched from my gums. Hot blood ran down my chin as my face began to shift. "I drank three already."

Arlo was silent. Slowly, the blurry beige moon of his face turned red. Needle-sharp claws dug into my shoulder.

Good. He needed his true form if he hoped to handle me.

The blackness swelled. Fabric ripped as my spine lengthened, vertebrae snapping like popcorn. "Harper," I gasped, blood and sweat stinging my eyes.

A shadow fell over me, and Arlo's reply drifted from somewhere above my head. "I told you, Your Highness, I'll check on—"

"No," I growled, consciousness slipping. Words flitted through my mind, fire licking at vowels and consonants my new form didn't know how to make. But this was important. I couldn't have the female who smelled of honeysuckle and drove me crazy with her questions. And I couldn't release her. Not yet. But maybe I could please her. Make her hate me a little less.

The bones in my neck slid against each other, snapping veins like they were power lines. In a few more seconds, speech would be impossible.

"Cook," I gasped. "Let...cook."

The scent of brimstone filled my lungs. "Cook?" Arlo repeated, his voice guttural.

I grunted my assent. "Kitchen. Harp—" The knives snatched my breath away, but I dragged in more oxygen and tried again. "Let cook."

"Yes, sir. I understand. Leave it to me."

For a moment, relief replaced the pain and fire. With the last of my voice, I gave a final command.

"Get the chains."

CHAPTER
TWELVE
HARPER

Knocking woke me from yet another night of restless sleep. Blinking, I sat up and gazed around the shadowy bedroom. Through the sitting room's windows, the predawn sky was tinged with pink.

The events of the previous night rushed back, and my throat went dry as I swung my gaze back to the door. Oh god, what if Einar was on the other side of it?

Embarrassment curdled my stomach. How was I ever going to look him in the eye again? Although, maybe that had been Einar's intention all along. He'd witnessed me at my most vulnerable. Maybe he'd scooped me from the kitchen floor and carried me to bed on purpose, knowing I'd hide in my room for the remainder of my stay at Draithmere. Hell, he might have orchestrated the whole scene with the centaurs. Set me up to get blindsided by lust so powerful I would have done anything to assuage it.

It was a devious thing to do. Smart, but devious.

The knock rang out again. "Miss Ward?" Arlo called through the door. "I apologize for waking you so early."

Relief swirled through me, along with another dollop of embarrassment. Arlo was no fool. Even if Einar hadn't shared what happened in my bedroom, the steward had almost certainly filled in the blanks. But Arlo had been a gentleman about the ordeal. He'd delivered my dinner later than usual last night, explaining he'd been tied up with "estate accounting issues" that left him scrambling to throw together a quick and easy meal. It was a plausible enough excuse, but we both knew he was just being polite by ignoring the incident with the centaurs. By some unspoken agreement, neither of us mentioned the scene in the kitchen, and I'd grabbed the food and practically shut the door in Arlo's face.

"Miss Ward?"

I cleared my throat. "It's all right."

A pause. Then, "Could you open the door? I have a proposal for you."

I sat up straighter. A proposal? For a second, I contemplated shouting the question through the door. But Arlo's knocking was just a formality. If he truly wanted to enter, I had a feeling nothing could stop him.

"Just a minute," I called, sliding from bed. I threw on the first clothes I could find, then opened the door.

"Good morning," Arlo said. In dress pants and a gleaming white oxford, he looked like he just stepped out of a corporate board meeting. His expression brightened as he looked past me. "Oh good, you ate the grilled cheese."

I turned, following his gaze to the table where I'd left the dinner tray.

"I hope it wasn't cold," Arlo added.

"It wasn't," I said, turning back to him. "And even if it had been, I've been a college student for four years. I've eaten my share of cold grilled cheese."

Arlo offered one of his shy smiles. "It's hard to imagine a famous food critic's daughter settling for bad sandwiches."

Memories of Mom stirred, and a smile tugged at my lips. "My mother loved comfort food. One of her favorite diners served cottage fries smothered in ranch dressing, cheese, and bacon bits."

A look of mild horror crossed Arlo's features. "Ranch dressing? Miss Ward, there's no need to be vulgar."

My smile turned to laughter. "I know it sounds gross, but the flavor combination was magic. That diner had a line out the door at lunchtime."

Arlo tilted his head. "Do you think you could make those fries for me?"

"Right now?" I couldn't help looking over his shoulder to the hallway behind him, part of me expecting Einar to appear like a vengeful god.

"Prince Einar isn't here," Arlo said, clearly reading my expression. "He'll be away from Draithmere for several days while he attends to business."

A hollow feeling settled over me. Einar was gone? I was human leverage—his primary method for forcing my father's compliance. Einar had signed a contract to keep me. And now he just...left?

"Is everything all right, Miss Ward?"

I jolted. Arlo stared at me with soft brown eyes.

"Yes," I said. "Totally fine."

"So you'll make the fries?"

He was offering me access to the kitchen. Maybe I could make some of my mother's recipes. And I didn't have to worry about crossing Einar's path. On the other hand, Arlo was most definitely on heightened prisoner-sitting duty. As much as I would have liked to think he was interested in ranch-smothered cottage fries, I couldn't make myself believe it. He probably just wanted me someplace where he could keep an eye on me. But spending the day in the kitchen was better than being cooped up in my room.

"I'd love to," I said. "As long as you're okay with ranch."

Arlo sighed, but his eyes twinkled. "I suppose I can make an exception for you."

~

HOURS LATER, I STOOD AT THE SITTING ROOM WINDOW, MY GAZE ON the horizon as the setting sun slipped behind the mountains. My back was sore, flour smudged my shirt, and my cheeks ached from laughing at Arlo's subtle—and surprisingly raunchy—humor.

We'd worked amicably side by side in the kitchen, preparing breakfast and then an ambitious lunch that included a shepherd's pie from the recipes in my mother's notebook.

"Are we calling this shepherd's pie or hachis parmentier?" I asked, referencing the French version of the same dish.

Arlo gave the layers of ground beef, cheese, and mashed potatoes a critical look. "Hmm, I think it depends on what you're serving."

"What do you mean?" I gestured to the pie. "We're serving this."

"Oh no, Miss Ward, if you're using the French pronunciation for a potato casserole, you're definitely serving cunt."

Despite my best efforts, Arlo still refused to call me Harper. But he was getting there. We'd parted ways just before dinner, each of us carrying a dinner plate of leftover shepherd's pie and chocolate chunk and sea salt cookies. Arlo had work to do in the morning, but he'd given me free reign in the kitchen. *"Just don't go outside."*

The latter wasn't a problem. I shivered as I stared at the

maze. If I never met another pair of centaurs it would be too soon.

The last sliver of sunlight disappeared behind the mountains. Movement near the maze's entrance drew my attention. Goliath stepped from between two hedges, my corduroy jacket in his hand. He tipped his head back, his eyes locking onto me. His teeth gleamed white in his tattooed face as he lifted a hand and waved.

I waved back, my mood lifting at the sight of Goliath's cotton candy tail curling around his hip. He pointed at himself, then jabbed his finger toward the window, a question in his eyes.

"Me?" I mouthed, touching my chest. He shook his head, then flapped his arms like he was flying. He wanted to come upstairs. I looked at the bedroom door over my shoulder. When I turned back to the window, Goliath was gone. A second later, he stood beside me, a cloud of black smoke rolling around him. It rushed into my lungs, the scent like charcoal.

I spoke between coughs, my eyes watering. "How...do you... do that?"

Goliath waved my jacket around, the chain on his belt loop jingling as he dissipated the cloud. "I'm not sure, really. I can't remember a time when I wasn't able to morph." He handed me the jacket.

"Thanks." I draped the jacket over the back of the sofa. "Is that what it's called when you disappear and reappear? Morphing?"

Goliath nodded, his stubby horns catching the light. "Vampires can do it, too. I've heard rumors of a few witches with the gift, but I've never met one. Adina says it's possible but they're probably stealing powers."

"How would they do that?"

"By killing the supernatural with the gift and using their blood in a spell."

My gut clenched. "Would Adina—?"

"Nah. Adina's cool. She doesn't murder anyone unless they deserve it."

I frowned. "That's still not—"

"I wanted to bring your coat back, but I had another reason for coming." Goliath tipped his head toward the window. "I thought we might visit the maze again. Myrna finally returned. She feels really bad about scaring you, and she'd like to apologize."

I looked down at the maze, which now glowed under the light of a three quarter moon.

"Be a good girl and make yourself come."

Phantom desire curled low in my core. I couldn't risk venturing near the centaurs again.

I drew a deep breath as I met Goliath's gaze. "I appreciate the offer, but I can't. With Einar gone, Arlo is in charge. I don't want to do anything that might get him into trouble."

Disappointment washed over Goliath's features, but he nodded. "I get it. Arlo is a solid guy."

I smiled. "So are you, you know."

Goliath ducked his head. Under his swirling tattoos, pink dusted his cheekbones. "I don't know about that."

"Trust me." I crossed the room and grabbed the plate of cookies from the table next to the chair. "Do you think I give chocolate chunk and sea salt cookies to just anyone?"

Goliath's tail waved gently, the fuzzy tip bobbing. "I can't take all of those."

"Yes, you can. Trust me, I ate my weight in dough before they went into the oven. Take them to the maze. I've never made this recipe before, and I need some feedback. Really, you're doing me a favor."

Goliath grinned as he accepted the plate. "All right, Harper. I'll take them off your hands, but only for research purposes."

"Deal."

He left in another poof of smoke, and I went to the window and watched him reappear at the edge of the maze. With a parting wave, he stepped between the hedges and winked out of sight.

I stood at the window, my smile lingering as the sky slid from purple to a deep midnight blue. Goliath was so charming, it was hard to imagine anyone not liking him. But his inability to shift meant he had to hide in the maze.

"We're all here because we can't be anywhere else. We live peacefully. Draithmere is the only place where most of us can live at all."

And it was all because of Einar, the benevolent prince. But he'd been anything but benevolent toward me. On the contrary, he'd been arrogant and condescending. Dictatorial. And, last night, disgusted. Maybe he only extended kindness to magical creatures.

I turned from the window, a thought taking hold. Was it possible Einar disdained humans? He spoke of werewolves as inferior beings. Surely, humans were even less desirable. That had to be it. To him, I was a member of a lowly, mundane species with no magic. His lifespan might stretch half a millennium. Mine was unlikely to endure for a century. No wonder he'd been eager to leave my room after I orgasmed. My pleasure had probably repulsed him.

Follow the facts wherever they lead. Even if they were uncomfortable. Even if they led to pain.

But it didn't matter. Einar was gone, attending to "business" that was obviously an excuse to escape my company. The lofty prince of the lycans couldn't sully himself with a human.

Well, he didn't have to worry. If and when Einar returned, I'd stay in my room. And the last thing I told him remained true.

I hoped I never saw him again.

CHAPTER THIRTEEN

HARPER

One week later, my days had fallen into a pattern.

Every morning, I went downstairs and had coffee with Arlo. Then I cooked while he worked in his office, attending to various estate matters. We lunched on our own, then met for dinner, where we talked about everything from my time at Northwestern to Arlo's preferred accounting software. Conversations with the steward were relaxed and easy, although he remained tight-lipped about Einar's whereabouts. Every time I prodded Arlo for an estimated return date, his reply was always the same.

"The prince keeps his own schedule, Miss Ward. He could be gone for a week...or a month."

Goliath parroted a similar line when he visited me in the evenings. The diminutive dragon had taken to waiting for me in my room after dinner, which had quickly become my favorite part of the day. I gave him leftovers to share with everyone in the maze, and he regaled me with stories about the supernatural world and the beings who inhabited it. Goliath was an engaging and talented storyteller. He was also more forthcoming than Arlo, gifting me to tidbits that painted a vivid picture of a hidden world full of mystery and magic. It was a reporter's dream.

But after five days, my daily routine was getting old. I'd worked through all of my mother's recipes—and most of the ingredients in Draithmere's pantry. The refrigerator groaned with quiche, chicken fricassee, and consommé. Last night, Goliath had politely declined an apple pie, claiming even Rolfe couldn't keep up with the volume of desserts I'd sent to the maze.

And still, there was no sign of Einar. With each passing day, the curiosity that had plagued me all my life tugged harder. Did Einar's disgust run so deep that it kept him away for an entire week? Was he injured? Was he with someone?

I shoved the last thought aside as I made my way to the kitchen. Einar Rothkilde's personal life was none of my business. Although, it was hard to imagine any woman putting up with his ever-changing moods. And his imperiousness. And stubbornness. The man had zero good qualities.

Arlo wasn't in the kitchen when I entered. For a moment, I considered looking for him, but a glance at the calendar tacked to a bulletin board near the butler's pantry revealed it was Saturday. He was probably sleeping in.

I gnawed at my lip as I considered my options. Coffee was top of the list, of course. But breakfast was going to be difficult to pull off. We were out of eggs, and I'd used the last of the flour for the apple pie. If I could find some powdered pancake mix, I only needed water.

"Sorry, Mom," I mumbled, imagining my mother's horrified expression. My hopes were low as I entered the pantry. Considering how many recipes I'd run through over the past week, I'd be lucky to find—

I stopped, shock rooting me to the floor. The pantry was

fully restocked, the shelves groaning with supplies. A row of tall, clear canisters held flour, sugar, and different kinds of dry pasta. Jars of spices marched in a line, along with boxes of crackers and cookies. I drifted forward, my gaze on a large bag of coffee beans. Obviously, Arlo had gone for a grocery run while I slept.

A *massive* grocery run. It must have taken hours. Instinctively, I grabbed a box of graham crackers, intending to turn the label outward.

But it was already out. My breath caught as I stepped back and surveyed the shelves. *Every* label faced outward. Every box, canister, and jar was perfectly aligned. Just the way I would have arranged them.

"Oh, good, you found the groceries."

I turned to find Arlo in the pantry doorway, his clothes as impeccable as always. A satisfied expression glimmered in his eyes as he gazed at the shelves.

"You didn't have to do all this," I said.

He blinked. "I didn't."

"But...you had to. We ran out of everything."

"I didn't buy groceries, Miss Ward. Prince Einar did."

My heart skipped a beat. "He's back?"

"Yes, he arrived late last night." Arlo ran his gaze over the shelves. "Were you looking for something in particular?"

"Pancake mix, but it's not a big deal."

Arlo reached behind his back, then produced a box of powdered pancake mix with a golden-brown stack dripping with syrup on the front. "Will this do?"

"What are you?" I blurted. Instant heat flooded my face. "I'm sorry. Maybe it's rude to ask."

A smile warmed Arlo's eyes. "It's okay. I wouldn't have allowed you to see my magic if I minded you knowing what I am." Suddenly, a ghostly pair of large, black horns flickered on either side of his head. His skin reddened, and his voice grew deeper as he tapped his chest. "I'm a Legerdemain demon." He pulled a pink rose from thin air, then extended it toward me. "My people can retrieve items from other planes. Like a magical sleight of hand."

Awe spread through me as I accepted the rose. Unable to resist, I buried my nose in its petals. "That's such a cool power."

Pain flitted through Arlo's eyes. "Not everyone thinks so. Traditionally, my kind work as assassins. We can pull weapons from anywhere, which makes us excellent killers. Few in the supernatural world trust us. Most fear us. More often than not, we're shunned."

My heart sank. I stepped close and put a hand on his arm. "Oh, Arlo. What about other Legerdemain demons? Do you have a community you can rely on?"

His mouth twisted in a bitter smile. "I'm afraid not. All demons are long-lived, and most clans are old-fashioned." He gave a short, humorless laugh. "Archaic is probably a better word, to be honest. The elders prize strength and brutality." He drew a deep breath and looked me straight in the eye. "Demon strongholds aren't an easy place to be gay."

My throat thickened. Before I even realized what I was doing, I'd yanked him into a hug. He stiffened, and for a second I thought he'd pull away. But he placed the pancake box on the shelf beside us and then rested his chin on my shoulder.

"I'm not sad about it anymore," he murmured. "I never wanted to be an assassin anyway."

I eased back so I could see his face. "I'm really glad you're not an assassin. And I'm honored to call you a friend."

His brown eyes shimmered with moisture. "Me too."

"Does that mean you'll finally start calling me Harper?"

"I promise to think about it, Miss Ward." He straightened,

glowed more brightly. The letters were thick and ornate—and definitely not English.

A sound at my back made me whip around. Einar stood in the doorway, his wide shoulders filling the frame. His eyes gleamed like pewter, and his dark blond hair looked damp as if he'd just come from the shower. The faintest hint of forest and leather teased my lungs.

"Harper," Einar said, his deep voice rumbling across the space between us. The two syllables of my name curled around me, caressing places I had no business thinking about.

"I..." I swallowed against a dry throat, his penetrating stare doing odd things to my stomach. "I was just..."

"You were curious." He closed the space between us, his eyes holding something...soft. Before I could figure it out, he stopped beside me, his large frame casting a shadow over the desk. "But it's dangerous to be curious about this book."

I tore my gaze off him long enough to look at the glowing letters. The long, elegant swirls seemed to shimmer and dance like a mirage in the desert. "Why?"

He stared down at the book, his features even more rugged in profile. "It displays itself differently to each person. Whatever entices you the most is what you'll see." Slowly, he reached out and touched a fingertip to the edge of the leather. The book rippled like the surface of a lake, the silver letters wavering and then reforming.

Goosebumps pebbled my skin. Every time I thought I was used to magic, something new surprised me.

I looked at Einar. "Why is that a bad thing?"

Einar met my gaze. "The book gains power when it's read. If you read long enough, it will show you whatever knowledge your heart desires. But there's a catch. Over time, its magic has evolved to make you so engrossed you'll start reading and never stop. To open it is to risk surrendering to its power. People have wasted away in front of it."

Wariness drifted through me. "Why do you have it?"

A teasing look entered his eyes. "I think you'll agree I could stand to use a little more knowledge."

Wait. Was he flirting with me? "Aren't you afraid it'll trap you?"

His gaze dipped to my mouth. Maybe it was a trick of the light, but gold appeared to flicker through his eyes. "Are you worried about me?"

My breath caught. "No," I said, my voice husky in my ears. Warmth spread through me, echoes of lust teasing at my nipples and the sensitive places between my legs. I throbbed there, heat building.

Einar lifted his gaze to mine. A knowing, challenging look glinted in the gold-sheened depths. "Ah, Miss Ward. I smell a lie."

CHAPTER
FOURTEEN
EINAR

Harper gave a little gasp, her blue eyes flaring wide as lust swirled between us. “You called me Harper before.”

My dick tightened. When I’d sensed her in my study, I told myself I was going to keep things quick and impersonal. Five days away should have been plenty to clear her from my system. To cure the need that plagued me whenever she was near.

It wasn’t. As the sweet scent of her arousal invaded my lungs, I knew that a hundred years wasn’t enough time to purge my need. But five days was long enough for me to control the parts of me she couldn’t see. Those parts had to stay hidden. If I’d been a better man, I would have stayed away forever. That would have kept her safe. But I wasn’t that good of a man, and I couldn’t make myself walk away. Not now.

I wanted her too badly.

More importantly, she wanted me too. And this time, centaurs had nothing to do with it. For some inexplicable, miraculous reason, Harper was just as caught up in me as I was in her. Had the attraction been there all along? What brought it out? Whatever it was, I wasn't going to look too hard at it. Not with her standing before me, her luscious body throwing off enough heat to set my hair on fire.

"Did I?" I murmured, ignoring the way the Book of Crubeus rippled and changed shape in my peripheral vision. The woman in front of me was far more tempting. Helpless to resist her, I stepped close and feathered a thumb over her plump bottom lip. "And do you prefer it when I call you Harper?"

Her shaky exhale fluttered over my fingers. "Yes." She seemed frozen—and more than a little flustered—but she didn't pull away. "What are you doing?"

"I could ask you the same question." I made another pass with my thumb. "You came looking for me. Or maybe you just wanted to snoop in my study."

Her blue eyes flashed. Like always, the little flare of irritation went straight to my cock. "I wasn't snooping," she said.

"So you were looking for me." I let a smile curve my lips. "You wanted to see me."

Her thick, dark lashes lowered as she looked at my mouth. "I..."

Taking a chance, I slid my hand to her jaw—and had to suppress a groan at the silky feel of her skin against my palm.

Her heart sped up, the pulse in her throat fluttering like a trapped bird. "Arlo said it was your idea to let me use the kitchen while you were away."

A week ago, I might have denied it. Let her think my steward was trying to keep her busy. But the arrangement had obviously pleased her, so I'd be damned if I didn't take credit for it.

"It was," I said. "You mentioned wanting to make your mother's recipes. I thought this was a perfect opportunity."

Her gaze softened. "It was."

"Then I'm glad. Harper."

The scent of her desire thickened, the air heavy with honeysuckle and a deeper, headier perfume that was hers alone. Pink bloomed in her cheeks. "You went grocery shopping for me."

"Yes."

"You replaced all the ingredients I used and then some."

"I did."

She searched my gaze, something both hopeful and solemn in her eyes. "Why would you do that?" she whispered.

Electricity sparked between us, the little currents licking at my skin. I was done lying to myself—and to her.

I lifted my free hand to her cheek so I was cupping her face with both hands. "You're a reporter, Harper. Haven't you figured it out by now?" Unable to help myself, I stroked a lock of bright hair away from her face. "I thought five days away would fix this, but I was wrong."

Her lips parted. She stared up at me with blue eyes filling with something like wonder. "Fix what?"

"I want you. You're under my skin, Harper Ward. And the harder I try to fight it, the more I want to make you mine. No one challenges me like you do. No one dares. Every time we argue, I walk away wondering if I should have kissed you instead."

Her breath caught, the wonder in her eyes growing. "You don't hate humans?"

Surprise flared in my mind. Although, maybe it shouldn't have. I hadn't really given her a reason to think I held her species in high regard. *Time to remedy that right fucking now.*

I brushed the pad of my thumb over the spray of freckles on her nose. "I don't hate humans. In fact, I find myself utterly entranced by this one."

"I thought..." She trailed off, a deeper pink staining her

cheeks. The color should have clashed with her hair. Instead, it made those charming freckles glow like little specks of gold.

Gods, the woman checked all my boxes. "What did you think?" I asked.

"I thought maybe you were disgusted when I..." She swallowed, and her voice went low. "When I orgasmed in my room."

For a second, I was speechless. Then I canted her head back, forcing her to hold my gaze. "Harper, *disgust* isn't a word in my vocabulary when it comes to you. I haven't stopped thinking about that day, or how fucking perfect you looked."

"But...you left. You walked out like you couldn't wait to get away from me."

"Because I was going to fuck you if I stayed. And it seemed like you didn't want that. You said as much."

She bit her lip, the gesture making more blood pump to my dick. A mix of humor and desire shimmered in her eyes. "I guess we're both really stubborn."

"Probably. You're worse, though."

She huffed a laugh, and my heart soared at the opportunity to be silly with her. To joke with the woman who drove me mad in the best possible way. "Our communication skills could use some work," she said.

I stroked her cheeks with my thumbs. "Fair enough. I'll go first. Your scent is in my lungs. I want it on my tongue."

A tiny whimper escaped her. The scent in question swirled thicker, her sweet essence perfuming the air.

"Maybe we should try that," I offered, sliding a hand lower and tracing her delicate jawline.

The pulse in her neck fluttered more wildly. Her nipples thrust against her sweater. *Another sweater.* The thinnest one yet.

"Maybe we should," she breathed.

It was all the permission I needed. In a blink, my hands were on her hips, her gasp in my ears as I swung her onto the desk. I deposited her on the edge, shoving the Book of Crubeus out of the way in the process. It flopped open, its gleaming white pages laid bare. Lines of ancient text flowed down the parchment. Whispers followed in their wake.

Harper started to look over her shoulder.

"Don't," I said, catching her chin and forcing her head back around.

"The book!" she protested. "It'll trap you."

Stepping between her legs, I reached around her and flipped the book closed. "I'm strong enough to resist it. But damn if I can resist you."

Grasping her chin, I bent and kissed her. She opened under me right away, her lips warm and soft. And she tasted as sweet as I'd imagined, the honeyed nectar of her tongue driving my lust higher. Deepening the kiss, I swept my hands up her sides, roaming her curves. She dug her fingers into my shoulders and yanked me closer. With a hungry-sounding moan, she hooked a leg around my hip.

I grasped her thigh and bore her back, laying her out on the desk. She arched into me with another moan that went straight to my dick. Still kissing her, I slipped a hand under her sweater and worked my way up, mapping the dips and curves of her delicate ribcage before reaching one firm breast. Her nipple strained against the thin fabric of her lacy bra. I plucked at the eager point, then rolled it between my thumb and forefinger.

Harper gasped into my mouth, her body bowing off the desk. She tangled a hand in my hair, tugging at the strands as I broke the kiss to trail my lips down her neck. When I reached her pulse, I flicked my tongue over the frantic beat.

She made a needy sound as she cradled my head against her. "Please. Please, Einar."

My name on her lips was the sweetest sound anyone had ever uttered. *She* was sweet. And I needed more of her.

I lifted my head and met her gaze. "I need to taste you." On the remote chance my meaning was unclear, I moved my hand to the button of her jeans. "I want to eat your pussy, Harper." Her eyes went wide, her irises darkening with desire.

I slid my fingers down, stroking over the denim that covered her sex. She was so wet she'd almost soaked through the fabric. "I want this," I said, hearing the growl in my voice. "I want to bury my face between your legs and lick you until you scream. I want every drop of honey, sweetheart. Say yes."

She gave a shaky nod. "Yes."

Triumph surged through me. I stripped her jeans off—and then caught my breath at the sight of her in nothing but panties and her thin sweater. She was like a creamy dessert, her strawberry blond hair spread on my desk and her pale skin glowing against the wood. But it was her pussy that held my attention. The flimsy, cream-colored silk between her legs clung to her folds, the sweet furrow between them dark with arousal.

I met Harper's stare. "Grip the edge of the desk."

Her breasts rose and fell rapidly. She licked her lips, hesitation in her blue eyes. "Why?"

I smoothed my hands up her legs, urging her knees up and placing her feet flat on the desk. She moaned as I lowered my head and licked the damp silk that covered her opening. Her salty-sweet taste teased my tongue.

And it wasn't nearly enough.

"Because," I said, slipping my fingers under the silk—and almost losing my mind at the damp, hot feel of her most intimate skin against my hand. "I have a feeling this pussy of yours is going to taste like candy. When I find something sweet, I take my time with it. So you're probably going to need to hang on." With one swift motion, I ripped the panties from her body.

Her gasp echoed around the study as I went to my knees and yanked her ass to the edge of the desk. Then I spread her pussy with my thumbs and ran my tongue up her center. *Ecstasy.* She was ambrosia, her cunt as sweet and intoxicating as I'd imagined. Moisture pooled at her entrance, the sight of her creamy, pink perfection instantly searing itself into my brain. Spreading her wider, I thrust my tongue inside her.

The desk creaked as Harper trembled above me, her breathless sounds of surprise becoming impassioned moans. "Oh my... Oh god, *yes*. Yes, Einar." Her knees fell wide, and she squirmed against my mouth.

My hunger grew, a growl rumbling in my throat as I laved her slit, drawing forth more of her silky sweet arousal. I lapped and sucked, running my tongue over her plump lips before fucking her with my tongue.

Her soft moans filled my ears as she writhed on the desk. A second later, pain shot through my scalp as she gripped my hair and dragged my mouth to her clit.

"There," she growled, holding me where she wanted me.

Yes, ma'am. I circled her clit with my tongue, teasing the swollen little bud.

"Yes, yes," she panted, bucking her hips against my face. The desk creaked rhythmically with her thrusts. Her moans grew louder, her movements more frantic. I sucked at her clit, bracing for her to come.

"Where have you been the past five days?" she asked.

I paused, surprise and amusement coursing through me in equal measure. Finally, I turned my head and nipped at her inner thigh, making her yelp. "Is this some new reporting tactic? Offering me a taste of paradise while you pepper me with questions?" I fluttered my tongue over her clit.

"Oh god," she moaned, her legs trembling around my ears. "Is it working?"

I couldn't hold back my chuckle. "No." I pushed a finger inside her, and I couldn't control my groan when her pussy clamped down. "Stop being nosy and come on my face." Pumping my finger inside her, I fastened my mouth over her clit and sucked hard.

"Oh!" She tightened her grip on my hair, ensuring I couldn't move. Not that I would have moved for anything. I sucked and licked down her folds, dropping kisses over her slick, feverish flesh before returning to her clit. The next time I suckled the questing bud, her cries rose to a wail.

"I'm coming! Oh my... Einar, I'm coming!" She stiffened, her cries climbing as she claimed her pleasure.

I took her through it, suckling her clit and pumping my finger into her tight, pulsing passage. Dragging forth every last drop of pleasure.

Finally, she went limp, her satisfied-sounding sigh fluttering around my ears. I stood and wiped my face. Then I pulled her up and threaded my hands through her hair. She was breathless, her temples damp and her cheeks bright pink. I wanted to keep going—to press her back down, free my cock, and plunge into her heat.

As if she'd read my mind, she regarded me with glassy, lust-drunk eyes. "What about you?"

I pulled a strand of hair from her sweaty forehead and smoothed it back. "What about me?"

Something vulnerable flashed in her eyes—there and gone so quickly I wouldn't have caught it if I hadn't been standing so close. "Don't you want to keep going?" she asked.

I took one of her hands and guided it to my erection. As her eyes rounded, I gave her what I knew was a rueful smile. "You have no idea how much I want to keep going." I rested my forehead against hers. "But you deserve better than a desk or a sofa in my study. When I fuck you, Harper, it's going to be in my bed, where I can spread you over my face and eat your pussy properly."

Her eyes darkened to sapphire. Her reply was a thread of sound. "That wasn't proper just now?"

"Not at all. That was a warm up." I slipped a hand between us and pushed two fingers into her heat. Her pussy clenched around me, and she shivered, her eyes locked with mine even as her flush stole down her neck.

I smiled. "As I said before, when I find something sweet, I like to take my time with it. So that's how we'll start. And when you're slick and begging, I'll give this pussy what it deserves." Slowly, I slid my fingers in and out, finger-fucking her without touching her clit. The thick, wet sounds of her juices warred with her ragged breaths. I continued pumping my fingers into her heat. "Now, I couldn't help but notice you loaded up my refrigerator with food. Are you going to feed me?"

Her reply came in a breathless rush. "Do you...oh god... want that?"

"Mmm, I definitely do. How about dinner tonight? You cook. I'll clean."

"Do princes clean up after dinner?"

I withdrew my fingers enough to circle her clit, and I smiled when she shivered and dug her teeth into her lip. "This one does," I said. "Have dinner with me, Harper."

She nodded, her eyes glittering with lust. "All right."

"Good." I pulled my fingers from her pussy, and she gave a little cry of protest as I tugged her off the desk and set her on her feet. I took a moment to steady her, and then I moved briskly, retrieving her jeans and ruined panties from the floor. She blushed furiously as I tucked the panties in my pocket, and she made an exasperated sound when I crouched before her with the jeans.

"I can do it," she huffed, but she let me help her into her pants, and she stood docilely as I straightened her sweater and smoothed her hair.

"There," I said, stepping back. I sucked my fingers into my mouth, and I didn't muffle my growl as her taste hit my tongue again.

Despite everything we'd done over the past half hour, Harper's cheeks went scarlet. Her hand shook as she tucked a lock of tangled hair behind her ear.

I licked the last of her arousal from my fingers. Then, with a hand on her shoulder, I turned her toward the door and delivered a firm swat on her ass. "You're distracting me, woman. Go back to the kitchen and make my dinner."

She rounded on me, one hand going to her posterior. As I skirted my desk and settled in my chair, it was clear she didn't know whether to be angry or amused. She seemed to settle somewhere in the middle as she shot me a disgruntled look.

"What do you like to eat?" The second the words left her, she snapped her mouth shut, clearly realizing what she'd said.

I leaned back in my chair, anticipation flaring under my skin. "Harper," I said, loading my tone with as much suggestion as possible. "If you make it, I'll eat it."

She absorbed the double meaning with bright pink cheeks and a jerky nod. Then she was gone. But I had her panties in my pocket. If dinner went the way I planned, I'd soon have her in my bed. And if a little voice in the back of my head warned the latter was a very bad idea, I didn't hear it.

I pulled the Book of Crubeus in front of me, flipped it open, and resumed searching for the elusive knowledge that might finally deliver the freedom I'd waited almost a century to find.

CHAPTER FIFTEEN

HARPER

"You look beautiful," Einar said, his eyes gleaming in the candlelight.

We sat in Draithmere's dining room, which boasted the kind of high-quality antiques my mother would have swooned over. But I hardly noticed the elegant hutch and scroll back chairs.

No, my attention was occupied with the roguishly handsome lycan prince at the head of the table. Einar had seated me to his right, which meant we didn't have to shout to hear each other.

And he hadn't taken his eyes off me—not even when Arlo brought in the crab bisque I made as a first course.

"Thank you," I said now, glancing down at my dress, which was the only one I'd brought from home. Alone in my room before dinner, I'd hesitated to wear it, thinking it might be too much. That maybe I'd look too eager—or, worse, desperate. But those fears had evaporated when I saw Einar.

He was every inch a prince in a dark suit that molded to his body so lovingly it had to be bespoke. He'd gone without a tie, and his starched dress shirt was open at the collar, revealing a tantalizing vee of golden skin. Silver cufflinks winked at his wrists. His dark blond hair was brushed back from his forehead, and he smelled expensive, like cologne sprinkled over pinecones.

"That dress suits you," he said, sipping from his wineglass. His silver eyes made a quick sprint down my bodice. "Armani?"

Surprise tripped through me. Although, maybe it shouldn't have. Einar clearly knew fine things.

I smoothed a hand down my skirt. "Yes. Several years out of style, I'm afraid."

"Couture never goes out of style." Einar toyed with his wineglass, his long fingers caressing the stem. A thick, silver watch peeked from under his cuff. "But you could wear a potato sack, and no one could take their eyes off you. Including me."

The heat that had simmered between us since we sat down sizzled higher. A second later, Arlo swept into the room with two dinner plates in his hands.

"Chicken piccata over linguine," he announced. He moved quickly, placing the plates in front of us and then disappearing as swiftly as he'd appeared. When I turned my attention back to Einar, he watched me with an intensity that let me know he'd never stopped.

"I hope you like chicken piccata," I said, lifting my fork and knife.

Einar's eyes reflected the fire dancing atop the candles—and his expression was just as smoldering. "I already told you, sweetheart, I'll eat anything you make." He cut a piece of chicken and popped it into his mouth. His eyes widened, and he made an appreciative sound as he chewed and swallowed quickly. "Damn, Harper. You're a gifted chef."

Pride swelled my chest. "I'm glad you like it."

We spent the next few minutes eating, our conversation light and companionable. Einar seemed to take a genuine interest in the dishes I'd made, as well as the cooking I did with my mother growing up.

"She took me to several Michelin star restaurants when I was a kid," I said. "Unfortunately, I was too young to appreciate it, and I usually ended up ordering chicken fingers and macaroni and cheese."

Einar chuckled. "Was it good, though?"

"Yes. Looking back, it didn't matter what I ate. The time spent with her was more important. I think that's the main thing I took away from her work." I gestured to my plate. "Food isn't just about satisfying nutritional needs. It brings people together. Most of life's milestones revolve around it. We celebrate with it. My mom always said mealtimes were sacred for that reason."

Einar's gaze softened as he listened, his eyes holding a flicker of something deeper than mere politeness. "Your mother sounds like an amazing woman."

"She was," I said. My throat burned, and I quickly cast about for a change of subject before I embarrassed myself. My gaze landed on my plate, and I forced a laugh. "I think this is the first time in four years I've eaten off a surface that wasn't made of paper."

Einar gave me an assessing look. "You've struggled with money throughout your schooling."

Damn. So much for not embarrassing myself. I toyed with the last of my linguine. "It's been challenging, but I managed."

"Didn't your mother leave you a trust?"

I lowered my fork. "You know about that?"

His gaze was steady. "It's my job to know. As cliche as it sounds, knowledge is power. It's also protection. My world can't collide with yours, Harper."

In a blink, walls rose between us. The relaxed atmosphere faded, replaced with tension reminiscent of our earlier encounters. "You speak like we're on opposing sides of a war."

His expression turned thoughtful. "Throughout most of history, that hasn't been too far off from the truth. Humans have always feared the unknown. They create monsters to explain things they can't understand, and they use them as scapegoats for all sorts of human vices. When I was a young man, the world was a much crueler place than it is today. Disease was rampant. Death was everywhere. Vice was reviled in public and embraced in private. The poets and authors of the day incorporated that contradiction into their work, creating monsters that spread death while luring innocent humans into temptation."

He'd been a young man in the late Victoria era, and one monster had dominated that period of history. "Dracula?" I guessed.

Einar lifted his brows, mischief dancing in his eyes. "You've heard of him?"

His gentle teasing made my body light up, my nerve endings coming alive. "Vaguely," I said, my heart fluttering when he grinned, clearly enjoying our banter. "Is he real, or just a figment of Bram Stoker's imagination?"

"Purely literary, although vampires predate Mr. Stoker by at least a millennium. Stoker didn't break any new ground, but that doesn't matter. What matters is that he made vampires mainstream. For the first time, the average person in the street could read. Stoker's ideas spread. Soon, people were seeing vampires and werewolves around every corner. Then cameras arrived, and life for supernaturals became more difficult. The internet made it truly dangerous." Einar's chest lifted in a sigh. "The reality is, humanity is just one viral video away from learning they share the planet with magical creatures. If the truth gets out, and humans discover how powerful we are, they'll never stop trying to eradicate us."

Visions of Goliath and the others from the maze sprang into my mind. Already, they hid from their families because they were too different to fit in. How would the world react to someone like Leander, who burst into flames on a regular basis? Or Rolfe, who looked like an MMA fighter but was too tenderhearted to participate in his family's war? They hid in the maze because they couldn't survive in the outside world.

What about Einar? Had he created the maze to protect others, or did he have secrets of his own? The urge to dig for information sparked inside me. But for once, I didn't want to write a story. I didn't want to know for the sake of reporting. I just wanted to know more about him.

"How powerful are you?" I asked. "I saw you turn into a lycan. What else can you do that would make humans fear you?"

For a moment, silence reigned. I waited for him to dismiss the question, or perhaps accuse me of angling for information. Just as regret took hold, Einar's voice filled my head.

"I can speak without words."

I froze, my heart thumping hard. "You talked in my mind."

He nodded, and his voice flowed through my head like a river. *"Some claim it's what made my ancestors kings. Only those of my line possess the gift of telepathy. When I concentrate intensely, I can compel others to do my bidding in short bursts. But compulsion is very draining. It weakens me, so I don't do it very often."*

A sudden, mortifying thought occurred to me. "Can you tell what other people are thinking?"

"No," he said aloud, a spark of amusement entering his eyes. "Your thoughts are your own."

Relief flooded me, along with memories of all the times we'd bickered. He'd shopped for me. He'd lined up ingredients, the labels turned outward. He gave me the best orgasm of my life. And yet he made no mention of letting me go.

"How long are you going to keep me prisoner?" I asked.

He tensed, the movement subtle but there all the same. "I don't think of you as my prisoner, Harper. Not anymore."

With a glance at the dining room doorway, I pitched my voice low. "Because I let you go down on me?"

"Because I care about you," Einar said, anger springing into his eyes. His voice deepened. "Because I can't stop thinking about you. I've tried. For your sake, I've tried. But it's no good. Even now, I want nothing more than to strip that dress off and make you mine. On the floor. On the table. Against that wall over there. But what I really want is to see you in my bed. I don't want to own you, Harper. I want to own your pleasure."

I stared, my breath caught in my lungs.

"I want to make you come until you can't even think about leaving," he said in my mind. As he continued, his telepathic voice slid between my legs. *"I want to bury my cock inside you and make you scream my name until it's the only word you remember how to say."*

My inner muscles clenched, my body desperate for him to fulfill his promises. But he hadn't answered my original question.

I drew a deep breath. "Maybe I want that too, but not like this."

For the briefest moment, something wild and predatory peeked out from his eyes. He blinked, and it was gone, but the intensity of his silver stare was just as potent. "What does that mean?" he rumbled aloud.

"You signed a contract to keep me here against my will. As long as that agreement holds, we're not equals. If I can't leave Draithmere whenever I wish, I'm not truly free."

Gold flickered over his eyes, reminding me that the large,

beautiful man wrapped in expensive clothes was *not* human. He was one of the monsters he'd spoken of—a being mortals were meant to fear.

I waited, my heart in my throat, for Einar's next move. Maybe I'd ruined everything, destroying the connection between us before it had a chance to fully bloom. But I couldn't sleep with him if I couldn't even walk out the door.

"Arlo," he said quietly. A beat later, the steward entered the dining room. He stopped steps away from Einar, the teasing expression he'd worn earlier replaced with his usual reserve.

"Yes, Your Highness?"

"Please fetch the contract I signed with Orson Ward."

"Of course, sir." In one of his uncanny movements, Arlo reached into the air and produced a bundle of papers.

"Please show Harper her father's signature on the last page," Einar said.

I held my breath as Arlo flipped to the final page, then held it out for my inspection. Sure enough, my father's scribbled signature appeared next to Einar's.

"Thank you, Arlo," Einar said softly. Still holding my stare, he extended his hand. Arlo handed him the contract. Einar tore it in half, the rip of the paper almost shocking in the hushed dining room.

My heart raced as Einar tossed the ruined contract onto the table.

"That will be all, Arlo," he said. "Thank you."

"You're welcome, sir." The steward left, but not before I caught the smile that touched his lips.

When I returned my gaze to Einar, his silver eyes glittered with unconcealed desire. He rested one hand on the arm of his chair, his long fingers curled around the wood. The same fingers that had cradled my ankle as he wrapped my injury.

The same fingers he'd thrust inside me while he dabbled his tongue around my clit.

"You're no longer my prisoner, Harper," he said. "You can leave whenever you wish." He swallowed, the bob of his throat betraying his seemingly unflappable authority. "But I hope you'll stay."

Desire coursed through my limbs. He waited, the gauntlet cast between us. Now that he'd given me what I wanted, the next move was mine. Did I return to Chicago and put Einar behind me? Or did I accept his invitation and embrace the unknown?

The ruined contract lay on the table. Einar continued to wait, heat flickering in his eyes.

The future was up to me. All I had to do was tell him what I wanted.

"Take me upstairs," I said. "Do all the things you promised."

EINAR WAS ON ME IN SECONDS, PULLING ME FROM MY CHAIR AND swinging me into his arms.

"Arlo will see," I protested even as I curled my fingers into the sleek material of his suit jacket.

"Discretion is the hallmark of a good steward," Einar said. "Trust me, Arlo knows when to make himself scarce. We can be as loud as we wish. He won't hear us."

Einar carried me to a spacious suite decorated in dark, masculine colors. My heart stuttered as he settled me in the center of a massive canopied bed with a carved headboard. Eyes narrowed to silver slits, he stepped back and began to strip.

My throat went dry as I took in his muscular shoulders,

sculpted chest sprinkled with dark blond hair, and taut abs. When he dropped his pants, I sucked in a breath.

He wore no underwear, and his erection sprang long and thick from a tangle of curls a shade darker than his hair. The heavy sack underneath swayed as he kicked his pants aside, his golden body like a sculpture in an art museum. Clearly, the man never indulged in a cheat day. He was way out of my league.

"You're so fucking beautiful," he rasped, putting a knee on the bed and moving over me with reverence in his eyes. "I've wanted you since the moment I saw you. Did you know that?"

Wordlessly, I shook my head.

He flashed a quick smile as he pushed my skirt up my legs. "That's probably a good thing." He smoothed a callused hand over my knee. "You make me helpless, Harper."

I shivered as his palm traveled higher, his fingertips teasing the sensitive skin of my inner thigh. His cock bobbed near my hip, the head round and dark with arousal. A thick bead of precome swelled from the slit. My mouth watered with the need to lift my head and press my lips there.

Well, why the hell not?

I followed my instincts, lifting onto my elbow and swiping my tongue over my target. Einar sucked in a breath. Then he cupped my chin in a warm hand and drew me gently upward so I faced him on my knees.

Narrowed, burning eyes met mine, and his growl rumbled the bed as he reached behind me and unzipped my dress in one precise movement. "You know what I think, sweetheart?" he murmured.

Lust blasted me as he pulled my dress over my head, leaving me in the skimpiest bra and panty set I owned. The black silk had been a rare splurge over the summer, when I earned a little extra money editing essays for students applying to grad programs on campus.

"No," I told Einar, licking my lips. His taste lingered there, salt and pine and a hint of something dark and spicy. I wanted more.

He unhooked my bra with a deft twist of his fingers, and his nostrils flared as my breasts sprang free. For a second, he seemed speechless, that little muscle ticking in his jaw. Then he cupped my breasts, one in each hand, and feathered his thumbs over my stiffened nipples.

"I think," he said, "you're a wicked girl under all your demure sweaters." He pinched my nipples, sending pleasure-pain spiraling through me.

"Yes," I gasped, arching into him. His hands were so big, his knuckles sprinkled with golden hair. The sight of his blunt, square nails scraping my nipples was surprisingly provocative.

He kept it up, twisting and pinching. Teasing and tormenting until my breathing went ragged and moisture soaked my panties.

Einar's nostrils flared. He pinched harder, wrenching another cry from me. "You know what else I think?"

"N-No."

"You didn't make me any dessert." He moved in a blur, gripping me around the waist and repositioning us so he stretched flat on his back and I straddled his chest. My head was still spinning when he ripped my panties from my body, grabbed my hips, and settled me directly over his face. His growl vibrated my clit and shot straight up my pussy. "So you owe me something sweet, love. And I'm going to clean my plate." He thrust his tongue inside me.

Deep.

I grabbed at the headboard, my eyes already watering from the things he was doing with his tongue. The pressure, the sounds. God, the *sounds*. His grunts and growls warred with the erotic smack of his lips and tongue working up and down every inch of my pussy.

"Fuck," I groaned, squeezing the headboard. "You keep ruining my underwear."

"Then stop wearing them," he said, his voice muffled. I wasn't sure how he could breathe—and I suddenly didn't care. My head tipped back of its own accord, and I gazed blearily at the bed's midnight blue canopy as Einar devoured me like a starving man who just discovered a feast.

My breath came in ragged gasps, my heart pounding so hard it threatened to burst through my ribcage. Pleasure spread from my pussy through every part of my body, my nerve endings electrified. My mind blanked. I couldn't think, couldn't do anything but cling to the headboard as Einar sped me toward rapture.

His stubble abraded my sensitive skin. When I squirmed, he dug his fingers into my hips and held me in place, working his tongue harder and faster.

"Yes!" I cried, a bonfire burning under my skin. I existed for this, just *this*, every part of me designed to receive pleasure.

Einar delivered. He flicked his tongue over my clit, his strokes hard and relentless. Pleasure built—a steady, persistent wave swelling and swelling. The world began to splinter. I was going to fly apart.

Einar moved his hands to my ass. Gripping each cheek, he spread me open and dipped his tongue to a place no one had ever touched me, let alone licked.

He licked. Hot and slippery, his tongue traced my puckered opening. It was deeply intimate. Intense and unexpected. Filthy and so, so fucking good.

"Yes," I breathed, squeezing the headboard. I rocked on his face, riding his tongue as he swirled it around and around my asshole, sending ribbons of wicked pleasure spiraling through me. Rushing me to the edge of something big and powerful.

He dug his fingers into my cheeks and spread me wider. Worshipping me even as he held me completely at his mercy.

"Oh god, oh god, oh god," I chanted, hanging by a thread. "I'm... Oh god, I'm com—" My words cut off as Einar flipped me under him in a dizzying display of speed and strength.

"Not yet, you're not," he rasped, pinning me to the bed with his weight. "You're coming with me, woman. I want this sweet pussy strangling my cock." He wedged his hips between my legs, but it wasn't necessary. I was already opening for him, my body *burning up* with the fires he'd stoked.

"Now," I panted, my hips rolling. I'd never been so aroused. He'd dangled an orgasm in front of me and then snatched it away. Now I was feral for it.

Bracing himself on one forearm, he gripped his shaft and stroked the swollen, leaking head up and down my cleft. "My kind are immune from disease," he said. "And I'm unlikely to get you pregnant, but—"

"I get the shot," I said. Although, maybe he wasn't familiar with modern medicine. "It's human birth control."

Amusement shone in his eyes as he continued his lazy, tormenting strokes. "I know what it is." He positioned himself at my opening and eased his hips forward, filling me by inches. Heat and pressure teased my passage. But I was finished being teased. I needed *more*.

Before I realized what I was doing, I'd gripped his jaw. "Then shut up and fuck me," I said, my voice guttural.

His answering growl was thick with approval. He entered me in one swift thrust.

I cried out, my inner muscles clamping around him. He'd prepped me thoroughly, but he still stretched me, his hard length leaving me no space of my own.

But I didn't want space. I just wanted him.

"More," I said, wrapping my legs around his waist. I pulled him tightly against me, and we both shuddered as his balls nestled against my ass.

A smile played around his mouth as he held himself still above me. Inside me. He traced my bottom lip with a rough thumb before trailing his fingers down my chest to cup one of my breasts. "So demanding, sweetheart. Who knew you'd be a little general in bed."

Raising one eyebrow, I squeezed my inner muscles around his dick. "And you're still talking."

Einar caught his breath. Then a mix of challenge and determination entered his eyes. Going to both forearms, he began to move, working his hips in a slow, sexy grind that grazed my clit.

Sparks sizzled through my veins. My lips parted on a low, breathy moan as I arched up to meet him, seeking more of that delicious friction.

"So tight," he murmured, maintaining his thorough, unhurried strokes. His chest hair grazed my breasts. The wet sound of his cock driving into me filled my ears. "Such a tight, hot cunt, Harper. Fuck, I'm going to need this pussy all the time."

He fucked me faster. The connection between us turned aggressive. Primal. It should have frightened me, but it didn't. On the contrary, it unlocked something just as primal within me. I reached up and dragged him down, pressing my mouth to his.

He took what I offered, sweeping his tongue into my mouth as he deepened his strokes. Our lips tangled. Our bodies slapped together. Every plunge of his cock sent more sparks cartwheeling through me.

Close. I was so close. Pleasure built once more, and this time I knew Einar and I would tumble over the wave together.

With a savage growl, he broke our kiss and pinned my arms above my head. Sweat flew from his forehead as he slammed into me over and over. So deep. The angle was perfect. Every thrust pounded against my clit. My orgasm gathered. I couldn't hold on.

"Einar!" I cried, my pussy already spasming.

"Right there with you," he grated. His fingers tightened on my wrists. He drove his hips forward one more time and then threw his head back, his roar splitting the air as he pumped inside me.

I flew into the heavens, my cry of ecstasy echoing in my ears. Thick, hot pleasure suffused me, scattering my thoughts into a million pieces. Nothing mattered. Nothing had *ever* mattered. Just this. And it kept coming, celestial waves shoving me farther and farther from shore. I floated, untethered from pain and the past.

But I had to return to earth eventually. When I fluttered back to myself, Einar was there, his big body stretched alongside mine. Turning to me, he tugged me against him and pressed his lips to my forehead.

"How do you feel?"

"Tired," I said. And sore. Sex with someone as big as Einar was its own kind of workout. I'd used muscles I never used before in my life.

He pulled back, an edge of wariness in his gaze. "Good tired or bad tired?"

I cupped his jaw. "The best kind of tired."

The shadows in his eyes fled, and his lips curved in a self-satisfied smile. "Too tired to hike with me tomorrow?"

He wanted to go on a hike with me? "Like, on a trail?"

His smile widened. "Yes, on a trail." He tucked a lock of hair behind my ear. “You’ve been cooped up inside. That’s my fault, and I’m sorry for it. I’d like to make amends.”

A man who apologized when he was wrong—and knew exactly what to do with a woman’s clitoris. Had I discovered a unicorn?

“Yes,” I heard myself say. “I mean, I don’t have any hiking gear, but...”

“Arlo will take care of it,” he said. “And if you get blisters, I’ll just carry you back to the house and fuck you better.”

An aftershock rippled through me. “I don’t think sex helps with blisters.”

Einar ran a fingertip over my bottom lip. He seemed fascinated with it. *Fine by me.* “I guess we’ll have to try it out,” he murmured.

“All right.”

He smiled. “So it’s a date.”

“It’s a date.” And maybe I’d gotten everything backward, and the hiking should have come before sex. Then again, I challenged anyone faced with an aroused Einar to decline a session on his desk...or in his bed.

He rolled on top of me and pushed his knee between my thighs. “It’s a long time until tomorrow, woman. I’ll have to keep you busy until then.”

CHAPTER SIXTEEN

EINAR

"Are you sure we're going the right way?" Harper asked, pausing to look at me over her shoulder. She wore her hair in two braids. Thick athletic tights molded to her hips and ass, and a signature tight sweater hugged her breasts. I didn't need hiking poles. My dick had kindly volunteered to take on the role.

"Einar?"

I realized I stood in the center of the trail, probably wearing a dumbfounded expression as Harper frowned at me. We'd been hiking for two hours, and we neared my favorite spot in the mountains. The breeze carried a sharp bite, but the sun was out, making the late afternoon air appear to sparkle.

I cleared my throat. "Sorry, did you ask a question?"

"Yes. I asked if we're going the right way." Harper looked around, her frown deepening. "There isn't much of a trail here."

That was an understatement. I'd worn a few trails into the ground over the years, but they weren't the smooth, manicured terrain Harper was probably used to. They were also narrow as hell.

"I know the mountain," I said. "If you veer off course, I'll tell you."

She grumbled as she faced forward and continued up the incline. "This would be a lot easier if you led us."

"And miss this view?" I asked, looking at her ass for the thousandth time since we left the house.

Okay, maybe the millionth.

She swung around again. "Is that why you insisted on bringing up the rear?"

I grinned.

She closed her eyes on a long blink. "Forget I said that."

I lunged forward and grabbed a handful of the rear in question. Leaning in, I let my lips graze the tender skin under her ear. "Sorry, sweetheart, but it's an unbeatable view." I squeezed her cheek, wishing I possessed the magic to make the layer of lycra separating us disappear. "Also, there's no way I can handle having you behind me. I'd spend all my time looking back to make sure you're okay and probably end up falling over a cliff."

Her soft laughter made joy flare in my chest. She pushed me away with a good-natured shove. "Fine. But this favorite spot of yours better be close."

Worry drifted through me. "Why? Are you getting blisters?"

"No, my boots are fine, I promise. But I'm not a lycan, and my stamina isn't the same as yours."

"Understood." I gestured toward the summit ahead. "We're almost there. Five more minutes."

With a nod, she turned and continued up the mountain. As I followed, her words burrowed into my mind. Because she was right. She was human—and like all humans, she was fragile. If she decided to stay at Draithmere, how much time would we have? A century?

My gut knotted. There had to be a way to extend Harper's lifespan. My brother's wife had been born human.

Yes, a voice in my head reminded me, *but Abby is a werewolf now.* Even isolated as I was, the news of my sister-in-law's miraculous transformation had reached me. Abby had survived a werewolf's bite—and, eventually, killed her attacker. Eschewing a thousand years of prejudice and tradition, Cyrus made her his queen. I didn't know all the details of my brother's relationship, but rumor had it he was enamored of his unconventional wife. And Cyrus was pushing two hundred years old. He probably didn't have to worry about Abby dying first.

Ahead, Harper crested the barely-there trail. A second later, she sucked in a breath. "Oh, my god, this is beautiful."

I moved beside her, and my negative thoughts dissipated as I caught sight of her expression. She gazed at the scenery before us, her cheeks pink from the cold and the exertion of the climb. The freckles on her nose sparkled like gold dust in the waning sunlight.

"What is this place?" she asked. "Is that a lake?"

"It's a hot spring," I said.

Harper jerked her gaze to mine. "That water is *warm*?"

"Very. You want to go in?"

She narrowed her eyes. "You planned this. You knew we'd have to skinny dip."

I tugged the end of one of her braids. "I may have hoped for it. I didn't think this spot could get any more beautiful, but seeing a certain redhead naked in that water is probably going to change my mind."

Lust glimmered in her eyes. Her full lips parted, and her breathing quickened. "I guess a quick dip wouldn't hurt."

"Wouldn't hurt a thing," I agreed.

Giggling like a pair of idiots, we stripped and waded into the water. Harper crowed with delight as she submerged herself.

"It's like bathwater!" she exclaimed, wading deeper. When the water reached her hips, she faced me.

And I couldn't contain my groan. She looked like a mermaid in the clear water, her taut nipples like two ripe berries. The spring lapped at her trim waist. Water invaded the sweet hollow of her navel.

"I've never been jealous of water until now," I said, staring at her luscious tits.

A devilish look entered her eyes as she waded to me. "I know the feeling," she said, spreading her palms over my chest. She pushed gently, guiding me toward the edge of the spring. I let her have her way, my heart speeding up with anticipation. My back hit the shore. Harper bit her lip as she trailed her hand to my dick.

"What are you doing?" I asked, a catch in my voice. The second she closed her fingers around my shaft, anything else I might have said drifted away. Now, I was probably capable of caveman grunts. Nothing more. Fine. Who needed speech, anyway?

Harper gazed up at me through the veil of her thick lashes. "I dreamed of this last night. Touching you. Putting my mouth on you."

Holy fuck. Somehow, I managed to form a coherent thought, and I let it flow from my mind to hers. *"I'm the one who's dreaming."* Her clever fingers plied my erection, sliding up and down, up and down. Cupping my balls briefly before returning to my shaft.

"Can I?" she whispered. "Will you let me suck you?"

I set a record reaching back and shoving my body from the

water. As I sprawled on the grass, she emerged after me, her body slick with water. The chill in the air didn't have much power with the heat rising from the spring. Not that it mattered. A snowstorm could have hit and I wouldn't have noticed. Not with Harper kneeling between my legs, one of her hands still pumping my dick.

"I love the way you look," she said, her blue eyes on my cockhead. She flicked her gaze up to mine. "I love the way you taste."

I'm dead. I've died and ended up in heaven somehow.

Water droplets glistened on Harper's breasts. More water clung to the tiny patch of strawberry blond curls between her legs. Forget mermaid. She was a siren. And she was all mine. Something wild and ancient within me lifted its head, its fangs bared at the thought of anyone taking this woman away from me. *Let them fucking try.*

With another sultry glance, Harper lowered her head and sucked my cock into her mouth.

My groan was probably loud enough to cause an avalanche. My mind went immediately hazy, my thoughts reduced to monosyllables.

Warm.

Wet.

Perfect.

Harper's mouth was all those things. She worked me slowly at first, licking and flicking her tongue over my cockhead as she continued to pump my shaft.

Another groan broke from me as I palmed her head. "Fuck yes, sweetheart," I said, guiding her up and down my cock. "Just like that."

She hummed, sending vibrations shooting down my dick to my balls. Her firm tits swayed with her movements. Her saliva slicked my shaft as she took me deeper and then bobbed her head.

My cock nudged the back of her throat. I tensed, worried about gagging her, but she kept going.

"Baby," I breathed, pleasure pumping through my veins. I stared at the nude goddess deep-throating my dick, disbelief warring with the desire blasting me like a blowtorch. Was this really happening? Maybe I'd fallen on the way to the spring and hit my head. I was unconscious on the side of the mountain right now, and this was a fantasy.

Harper moved her hands to my thighs, her slender fingers digging into the muscle. Her braids flew as she continued bobbing on my dick, her tongue slicking my shaft. My balls tightened. I was going to come.

But not yet.

I tightened my fingers in her hair. "Harper."

She released my dick with a *pop.* Panting, she gave me an anxious look. "Is everything all right?"

"It's fucking amazing. But I need to be inside you."

The worry fled her gaze. "Okay." She climbed up my body and straddled me, and I almost came on the spot at the sight of her plump, glossy cunt positioned over my straining cock.

"Fuck, this isn't going to take long," I muttered, gripping her waist. A meteor strike couldn't have pulled my gaze from the sight of her pussy swallowing my cockhead. The blunt tip stretched her opening, and then I was inside her, my dick surrounded by her searing hot clutch.

"Yes," she gasped, already rocking. Pink spread down her chest to the ruby-red tips of her breasts. "It feels so good."

I dug my heels into the ground and pumped my hips, bouncing her as I fought for control. "You like that? You needed a nice, big dick, didn't you, sweetheart?" She blushed harder at my filth, digging her teeth into her lip and threatening to make me go up in flames. "I can hear how much you want this," I continued. "Such a loud pussy. You've been wet all day, haven't you?"

"Uh-huh." She bounced harder, her hands on my chest and her head thrown back. Her braids swung wildly. Her tits jiggled, her puckered nipples dark with arousal. Mist rolled around us as we moved together, our moans and gasps joined by the gentle slap of water against the shore.

Harper's pussy strangled my shaft. Nothing had ever felt so good. As I'd predicted, I wasn't going to last.

I reached down and stroked Harper's clit, which swelled proudly from its little sheath. "Are you going to come all over this dick you wanted?"

She cried out, her movements growing more frantic. "Yes! God, yes, I'm going to come!"

"Let's see it, then, beautiful. Get my dick all wet. Soak it with that pretty pussy. Come on, baby." I rubbed her clit faster.

She came on a scream, her pussy clamping hard. My orgasm hit a second later, the force of it stealing my breath. I managed one more thrust before I seized Harper's hips and spurted inside her. She sagged over me, her pussy milking my cock dry.

"Holy shit," I panted, lifting her off me and rolling so we tangled together on the grass. We lay quietly for a moment, and then Harper lifted onto her elbow.

"Thank you for showing me the spring."

I flicked the end of the braid that dangled over her breast. "Showed you a good time, too."

She rolled her eyes, but her lips twitched. "So modest."

"Thank you. It's about time someone noticed."

Now, she laughed. "Please. I don't think your ego can get any bigger."

"When you're around, everything about me can get bigger."

I continued teasing her as we rinsed off and dressed. As we started back down the trail, I eyed her boots.

"Boots still good? Any blisters?"

"No blisters. Arlo did a good job picking out gear for me."

"Yeah. He has an excellent eye for that sort of thing."

Harper gave me one of her curious looks. "Can he really pull anything from anywhere?"

"He told you what he is?" It wasn't all that surprising. Arlo had displayed his gift in her presence often enough. And he liked her. Once he relaxed around people, he tended to open up.

"Yes," she said. "He also told me his people rejected him for being gay." Harper offered me a soft smile. "It was kind of you to give him a job."

I snorted. "It wasn't kindness. It was pure selfishness. Arlo is the best steward anyone could ask for."

Curiosity sparked more brightly in her eyes. "How did you meet him?"

A tendril of discomfort snaked through me. Arlo was a safe enough subject, but talking of him had the potential to lead the conversation down paths I wasn't quite ready to tread. But I had to tread them eventually. I knew that.

Just not right now. Not when things were so perfect.

"It was on this mountain, actually," I said. "About fifty years ago now."

"You've known Arlo for fifty years?"

"Yes. Watch that tree root." I guided her around a thick vein of wood protruding from the ground. "I'm sure Arlo told you that demons can be pretty backward in their thinking."

She nodded. "He said they're usually assassins."

"The Legerdemain are, yes. Arlo didn't want that life, and he wasn't going to settle down with a demoness like his parents wanted. So he found a place in the middle of nowhere and made camp." I smiled at Harper. "He definitely wasn't expecting me to stumble upon him. Literally. I tripped over him on a walk to the spring."

Harper put a hand over her mouth, her eyes twinkling above it. "He didn't know you lived here?"

"At the time, he was fresh from the demon plane and still jumpy around other people. He didn't venture out of the forest, so he had no idea Draithmere was just over the rise."

"So what happened?"

"I invited him to the house. It didn't take long for me to realize how much I needed a steward. And Arlo needed the protection Draithmere provides." I cleared my throat as I searched for a way to tell Arlo's story without divulging secrets I'd sworn to keep. "His people don't like it when one of their own leaves the nest, so to speak. They can be heavy-handed about forcing runaways back to the fold."

Harper made a soft, approving sound. "You gave him safety." She glanced at me. "The same as you did with Myrna."

The tendril of discomfort sprouted another shoot. "Did Arlo tell you about her, too?"

Harper kept her gaze on the trail. "A little. She lives in the maze?"

"Yes." I held my breath, waiting for Harper to keep digging. It was only natural for her to have questions about the maze. She'd seen the centaurs, after all. Of course she wanted to know what other manner of creatures lived among the hedges.

But Harper stayed silent. Grass crunched under our feet, and fingers of crisp wind tugged at our hair and clothes. We walked, content in each other's company, until the sun began to kiss the horizon. Eventually, Draithmere's chimneys came into view.

Finally, Harper stopped. As I halted beside her, she turned

to me. "You built the maze for supernatural beings who don't have a home."

I kept my expression as neutral as I could. "I have the space. Might as well do something with it."

"It was a good thing to do."

I didn't deserve her praise, but rejecting it meant opening myself to questions I wasn't prepared to answer. "It was no trouble."

Harper looked toward the mountain we'd just left. "Arlo came here to escape a future he didn't want."

"That's right."

She swung her gaze back to me. "Why did *you* come here?"

I startled, her question landing like a grenade lobbed at the center of my chest. She held my stare, her blue eyes clear and steady. Like any good journalist, she'd warmed me up, pitching softballs until she reached the destination she'd aimed for all along.

For a moment, the impulse to brush her off was almost too tempting to ignore. It would have been easier to order her back to the house. But it would destroy the fragile thing I'd built with her.

You'll destroy it anyway, a voice of reason reminded me.

Maybe. And I was a coward, because I wasn't ready to watch that progress burn. However, I had to give Harper something. A kernel of truth. She was too smart to back down completely.

I drew a deep breath. "I told you before that my brother is the king."

Harper nodded. "I remember."

"Cyrus and I had a falling out. It happened close to a century ago. I'm not proud of who I was when I was young. I was brash and hot-tempered." I slanted Harper a look. "In modern vernacular, I was a bit of a dick. My brother is a rule follower. He has to be. Lycan society is rigid." And I was stalling. I cleared my throat. "Cyrus is king, but he shares power with a Council of Nobles. I broke the law. I...hurt people, and I shouldn't have. Normally, the king would pass judgment on a criminal. But the council intervened, claiming Cyrus had a conflict of interest because I was a relative. They ruled against me, sentencing me to death."

Harper clutched her throat, her eyes going wide. "Oh my god."

"Obviously, I wasn't executed." I gave a bitter laugh. "Although, for a while, I wished those bastards had gone through with it."

"Don't say that," Harper murmured, her eyes sheened with tears.

I wanted to reach for her, but I forced my hands to stay at my sides. "Cyrus struck a bargain with the nobles. He banished me, cutting me off from lycan society. I'm not supposed to leave Draithmere."

Harper's eyes went wider. "But you came to Seattle. And you went to the grocery store for me."

"Yes. Technically, I broke the terms of my banishment. If the council wanted to punish me for it, they could. But I don't think that will happen. The nobles ignore me. My brother has done his best to forget I exist."

A tear slipped down Harper's cheek.

My heart squeezed. I caught the droplet on my finger. "Oh, sweetheart, please don't cry."

"I can't help it." She stepped into me and cupped my cheek. I waited for her to ask about my crimes. To demand what I'd done to merit such a harsh sentence. Instead, something fierce entered her eyes. "Whatever you did, it happened a century ago. It doesn't define you now. I know who you are. I don't need to know anything else."

I covered her hand with my own, my throat thickening. "I don't deserve you."

She shrugged. "Probably not."

We smiled at each other.

"Are you hungry?" she asked. "I can make us dinner."

I dragged her hand to my mouth and pressed a kiss in the center of her palm. "You make it, I'll eat it."

She held my hand the rest of the way back to Draithmere. And I tried to ignore the truth that pounded an insistent tattoo in my head.

I didn't deserve her.

And I couldn't lie to her forever.

CHAPTER SEVENTEEN

HARPER

Guilt dogged my steps as Einar and I entered Draithmere's kitchen.

He'd shared his secret with me. The least I could do was tell him I'd met Goliath and the others. I should have told him sooner, but the timing never seemed right.

Because I'd been busy enjoying myself on the receiving end of his tongue.

Heat flooded my cheeks. To hide it, I went to the fridge and peered inside. "Do you like chicken salad sandwiches?" I asked, raising my voice.

"As long as you have enough for ten of them," Einar said somewhere behind me. When I turned, a can of mayo in hand, he winked at me from the other side of the massive island in the center of the kitchen. "I burned a lot of calories today."

Well, at least now I had a reason for my flushed face. I pulled the rest of the ingredients from the fridge. As I arranged them on the island, Einar came to my side.

"How can I help? I'm pretty useless in the kitchen, but I can chop something."

I pointed to the celery. "You can chop that."

He got to work. I moved around the kitchen, gathering plates and forks. As I returned to the island, my gaze snagged on the moonlit maze visible through the patio doors. A fresh wave of guilt crashed through me. I had to tell him. The longer I dragged it out, the worse it was going to be. And why was I so reluctant, anyway? It wasn't like I did anything wrong.

Einar followed my gaze. Then he put a hand on my shoulder and turned me toward him. "You don't have to worry about the centaurs," he said, misinterpreting the source of my anxiety. "I'll make sure they don't bother you again. But it's still important to stay away from the maze. I know you're curious, but—"

"I met Goliath," I blurted. "And Leander and Adina. And Keir and Rolfe."

Einar stared. Then he stepped back, his expression shuttered. "When did this happen?"

"On my third night here. Goliath wanted to apologize for Myrna scaring me."

"Goliath said that?"

"Yes."

"Where did you meet him?"

"Well, he came to my room. Then he took me into the maze."

Einar's eyes flickered, going from silver to gold and back again. "He showed you the maze?"

Oh no. This was going exactly as I'd feared. "Yes, but it was no big deal. Everyone was lovely. Adina gave me tea and—" I sucked in a breath as Einar grabbed my arm.

"Adina gave you tea?" he growled.

"Yes, why?" I tugged at my arm, my heart speeding up.

Einar tightened his grip. "Did you eat anything?"

"Just cakes. Einar, please, you're hurting me."

"And you drank the tea?" He loomed over me, his features suddenly sharper.

Fear pumped like acid in my veins. What was wrong with him? "Yes."

His fingers bit into my arm, and I couldn't help my wince. "When?" he demanded.

"I don't know! It was days ago." I tugged harder. "Einar, let go of me."

He jerked me closer. "Last week? Just before you saw the centaurs outside?"

Was it? I racked my fear-addled brain. "Yes, it was the night before, but—"

He released me with a curse. Then he rounded the island and stalked to the patio doors.

Alarm bolted through me. "Einar!" I called, hurrying after him. "What are you doing?"

He ignored me as he flung the doors open and marched into the night. "Adina!" he bellowed. "Goliath! Show yourselves."

I ran down the patio steps, terror tightening my throat. "What's going on?" I asked, running to his side. "Why are you so angry?"

He rounded on me, rage blazing in his bright gold eyes. Fangs flashed as he spit his answer. "Because I don't like being taken for a fool."

"What?" I gasped, bewilderment joining my panic. "What are you talking about? No one thinks you're a fool."

Goliath stepped from the maze, his gaze darting from Einar to me. The hedges behind him rustled, and Adina appeared. Her mouth was compressed in a thin line, and she squeezed her hands together as she kept her stare pinned on the grass at her feet. The confident woman from the tea party was gone. Now, she appeared almost meek.

Einar stalked forward, stopping a few feet from the maze's entrance. His voice dropped an octave as he surveyed Goliath and Adina with furious eyes. "Explain yourselves. And don't fucking lie to me."

Goliath hung his head, his tail drooping. "It was my idea, Your Highness."

"No," Adina said, stepping to Goliath's shoulder. She lifted her chin, a resigned look in her eyes. "It was mine."

Goliath glanced at her. "We both played a role."

More confusion pummeled me. "What do you mean? What role?"

Goliath darted a look up at me before dropping his stare to the ground. "We, um, spiked your tea."

"Tell her the rest," Einar growled.

My heart pounded, a sense of doom gathering.

Adina met my gaze. "I infused it with a powerful potion designed to provoke extreme lust. And then I bribed the centaurs to put you in Prince Einar's path so you wouldn't suspect anything."

My stomach dropped.

"It was my idea," Goliath repeated, his voice thick with emotion. He shifted from foot to foot, and he looked miserable as he spread his hands. "You wrote about Prince Einar in your book, and I thought—"

"You read my notebook?" I demanded. Angry tears burned my eyes. "You put drugs in my tea?" My stomach lurched. Oh god, I was going to be sick. "I thought you were my friends."

"We are!" Goliath cried, his eyes gleaming with moisture. "We never meant any harm."

Einar barked a short, humorless laugh. "Well, you've caused plenty." He looked at Adina. "Manipulating emotion is a crime on every plane. I should toss you from Draithmere and let the law of your coven catch up to you."

Adina blanched. "You wouldn't."

Einar's voice went impossibly low. "I should—" He made a choking sound. The skin on his neck rippled. He dragged in a breath. "I should..."

My alarm grew. Something was wrong with him.

Goliath cast a worried look around the lawn. "Where's Arlo?"

Einar snapped his jaws, making Goliath jump backward. Adina gasped and then clutched Goliath against her side. "I rule here," Einar snarled, his words garbled. "Not Arlo. Not anyone else."

"Of course, Your Highness," Goliath said, cringing away. He shot me a terrified look and mouthed, "Run."

Einar convulsed, his features warping and twisting. A bubble of flesh expanded on his cheek.

Nausea burned my throat. I backed away, horror and disbelief rising. Memories of the video I'd watched in my father's office surfaced. But that footage had showed Einar shifting into a sleek, powerful beast. This was different. His limbs contorted. Skin continued to bubble and stretch. A second later, a bubble on his neck burst, and blood soaked his shirt.

Adina slapped a hand over her mouth. Eyes wide with terror, she tugged Goliath backward.

"You won't..." Einar growled, lurching toward them. Chest heaving, he turned his head and spit blood onto the grass. He appeared to struggle to form words as he advanced on Goliath and Adina. "You won't...speak to Harper...again."

"W-We won't," Goliath said, shaking his head vigorously. He gripped Adina's hand as they continued retreating to the maze's entrance. The bog witch darted a look around.

"Arlo!" she shouted. "Arlo, hurry!"

Einar roared. A series of *cracks* rang out, and his head and shoulders shot upward like they were spring loaded. Suddenly, he was six inches taller. Fur rippled down his arms. More cracks, and his pants split open. Blood poured from a dozen wounds on his face and neck. His legs twisted, his kneecaps rotating to the sides. He opened a mouth full of pointed teeth and released an agonized scream.

"I'm here!" Arlo cried, sprinting from the side of the lawn. He skidded to a halt, his gaze on Einar. Then he looked at me.

"Go inside, Miss Ward. Now."

"I can't," I said, my heart racing. "We have to help him."

"And I will." Horns appeared on either side of Arlo's head. His skin turned ruddy...then crimson. His eyes glowed, and his features grew sinister. As he continued speaking, his voice dropped to an ominous rumble. "But you're in serious danger. Prince Einar is a rogue lycan. He can't control his beast. And once he loses control completely, he'll kill anyone he can get his claws on. Including you."

CHAPTER EIGHTEEN

EINAR

My control was a fraying rope. My vision blurred, darkness gathering at the edges.

Harper's face was a mask of terror as she watched my mangled shift.

Never wanted her to see it.

It was too late now. And if Arlo didn't hurry, it was going to be too late to save her.

"Go," I tried to tell him, but the word got lost in a roar. Deep inside my mind, my beast snapped more of its restraints. Harper paled, backing away from me. The present and past converged, all my secrets whipping through my deteriorating brain.

When I was a young man, my animal half and I had lived in harmony, sharing a mind and body.

And then everything changed. I started losing minutes and then hours. I fell asleep in one place and woke in another. Small animals around my family's estate went missing. The servants found bloodied clothing stuffed in the back of my closet.

I never remembered putting it there.

Until the fire came. It started as anger. At first, I could control it. Dismiss it. Someone insulted me, and I punched a hole in the wall. One of the assholes who sat on the Council of Nobles made an ill-timed quip—and then apologized profusely after I broke his jaw.

"He's a hothead," the other nobles whispered. *"The king's younger brother. It's normal for second sons to be resentful and brash."*

Those accusations were true. I resented Cyrus, my perfect older brother. Our mother's favorite. The golden heir with the laws of our forefathers tattooed on his arms. For years, I was content to be the playboy prince—irreverent and haughty. Cruel on occasion. I broke things because it was nothing to me that someone else had to fix them.

And then the fire came, and I was no longer brash. I was terrified. And I fought a losing battle. The gods punished me, I thought, and I prayed for mercy. I vowed to change my ways.

Mercy didn't come. The fire spread, burning away my reason. The next time I grew angry, the fire roared—and my beast responded.

I lost control. The two halves of my soul—man and lycan—splintered.

And the next time the servants found bloodied clothes in my closet, they found a corpse too.

Cyrus spared my life, but he couldn't secure my freedom. He sent me to the other side of the country, and he gave me money to buy land and build a house with enough protective spells to keep others out—and keep me in. Draithmere was a prison. My prison. I ruled a kingdom of rejects, my court full of jesters and broken people.

Coward though I was, I hadn't been completely dishonest with Harper. I'd met Arlo as I said, and I took him into my service because I was selfish and desperate. But Arlo wasn't just a steward. He was a warden—albeit one of my choosing. I was a convict and a rogue, yes, but I was still a prince, and I'd leveraged my title and position to strong-arm Cyrus into letting me hire Arlo. When the flames grew too intense, Arlo wrestled me into chains strong enough to hold me.

Over the years, he'd also used his considerable gifts to grant me temporary freedom from Draithmere's boundaries. The same magic that allowed Arlo to pull objects from different planes let him bend my prison's barriers just enough for short-lived reprieves. He smuggled me out of the mountains when I needed to deal with blackmailing journalists...or buy groceries. We rarely discussed his reasons for doing it. Maybe it was pity. Maybe it was wisdom. Someone had to keep the local werewolf packs in check. On my good days, I could do it—as long as I had Arlo to haul me back from the edge if I started to lose control. Whatever his motivations, he'd given me small snippets of freedom. And a purpose.

And he'd brought me Adina, who broke laws and created experimental potions that kept the fire at bay.

Except when it didn't. Sometimes, the witch's brew wasn't enough to squelch the fire. Like when my anger burned too high. Or when my lust flared too hot. Or when I discovered that the woman I wanted more than anything didn't really want me back. Adina's potions were potent and long-lasting. She and Goliath had orchestrated a romance based on deceit. Every moment of passion I'd shared with Harper was a lie. None of it was real.

I roared, the sound shaking the ground under my unsteady feet. Screams echoed around the lawn. Dimly, I was aware of more people rushing from the maze. Blurry shapes bobbed at the edges of my vision. Shouts rang out.

Harper. I had to get Harper to safety. Because she wasn't safe from me.

Fire licked at my ribs. Blood and sweat stung my eyes. I swung around, peering through the gathering darkness. Knives of pain stabbed at me. My bones continued to snap, my body caught between forms. The stench of wet fur invaded my lungs.

I opened my jaws to bellow for Arlo. Instead, I vomited a stream of blood and bile onto the grass.

A woman cried out. Honeysuckle caught in my nostrils. I lurched toward the scent, my consciousness slipping.

"No!" Harper screamed from somewhere to my right. "Let me go to him!"

Pain exploded in my head. *Skull split open.* It didn't matter. I had to make sure Arlo took Harper. She couldn't see me like this.

The clatter of hooves reached me. One of the centaurs had left the maze. More screams. Chaos reigned, the world a blurry mess of noise and color.

A yell trembled in my throat, but I lacked the vocal cords for human speech.

"Please!"

Harper again. The fire seared my chest, but I swung toward her, squinting through the darkness. A blurry red shape approached, and the scent of honeysuckle engulfed me. At the same time, hunger fired in my gut. My mouth watered, my beast clamoring for fresh meat. The scent of honeysuckle thickened. My fangs ached with the need to tear into flesh.

No. I stumbled back, desperate to put distance between Harper and me.

"Einar!"

Hunger clawed at my insides. My thoughts spun. The flames shot higher. Rage exploded.

Red. Red was the color of enemies.

Blindly, I slashed at my adversary.

A woman's sharp cry filled my ears. The rage receded. For a moment, clarity returned.

Arlo dashed across my vision in full demonic form. He bent and scooped something from the ground. *Harper.* Blood ran down her arm.

"We have to go, Miss Ward," Arlo said, his voice tight as he gathered her into his arms. Behind him, one of the centaurs herded a terrified-looking Rolfe into the maze.

Arlo swung toward me, giving me a glimpse of Harper's pale face. Our gazes collided. Her eyes were stark. Tears shone on her cheeks. She held her arm at an awkward angle, a red stain spreading over the sleeve of her sweater.

In some deep corner of my brain where I was still capable of regret, my telepathic gift sparked. Mustering the last of my power, I poured my heart into a final message.

"Forgive me."

Harper's eyes widened.

Arlo spun with her in his arms and sprinted toward the house.

The flames in my head roared. I was out of time. Lurching around, I loped across the lawn, leaving the maze behind. Knives of agony plunged deep into my muscles. The coppery taste of blood coated my throat. Halfway to the garage, I had to drop to all fours to keep running.

On contorted limbs, I half-ran, half-crawled to the garage. The latch on the main door was designed for me to enter with the swipe of a paw. Even so, metal shredded under my claws as I shoved inside.

The trap door to the safe room gleamed ahead, its edges spelled to emit enough light to draw me. In the old days, Arlo had propped the door with a rope and pulley system. Modern technology meant I only needed to press a button in the floor to spring the trap.

Rage roared in tandem with the fire in my head. For a second, I wavered, my thoughts a blinding whirlwind of pain and anger. But a single spark of reason still shimmered in the center of the encroaching darkness.

Harper. I had to keep Harper safe.

I bounded forward and hit the button in the floor. The trap door whisked open, revealing an inky abyss. A metal ladder offered a way down.

I didn't need it.

With a roar and the last of my consciousness, I flung myself into the darkness.

Where I belonged.

CHAPTER NINETEEN

HARPER

I was too numb to struggle as Arlo carried me into the house. Behind us, a frazzled-looking Leander and Goliath herded the rest of the maze's inhabitants into the hedges. Goliath cast me a final, sorrowful look over his shoulder before winking out of sight.

Arlo hurried across the kitchen and into the long hallway that led to the foyer.

"I can walk," I said, pushing at his chest. The pungent scent of sulfur burned my nose. The wound Einar had given me stung from my elbow to my wrist, but I ignored the pain. "Put me down. Please."

Arlo didn't look at me as he shook his head. "Not until you're safe." He took the stairs two at a time, carrying me effortlessly. It was difficult to reconcile the hulking, muscular demon who held me with the reserved, slightly built man I'd come to know. His horns curled against his hair, which was the same chocolate brown. Traces of his usual features remained under his prominent brow ridge and sharp cheekbones. But there was no mistaking him for anything other than a powerful supernatural.

We reached my room, and he sat me on my feet next to the bed. "I'll treat that wound, and then I need to see to Prince Einar."

"What happened downstairs?" I asked, cradling my injured arm to my chest. "What did you mean when you said Einar is a rogue lycan?" Even as the question left my lips, I knew the answer. Einar's transformation had been horrifying, his body seemingly trapped between two forms. When I ran to help him, he looked at me like he didn't recognize me.

And then he'd slashed my arm open. Madness had danced in his eyes, and he'd roared like he wanted to do a lot more than rake his claws over my skin.

Arlo reached for me. "I need to check your injury."

"It's fine," I said, pulling away. "Tell me what happened with Einar. No one has been honest with me since I got here. I deserve to know the truth."

Arlo's jaw tightened. Tension vibrated off him, but he gave a single nod. "Prince Einar lost control of his beast when he was a young man. It's always a tragedy when a lycan goes rogue. Usually, family members notice, and they intervene before disaster strikes."

Foreboding slid down my spine. "But that didn't happen with Einar?"

"No," Arlo murmured. "His Highness didn't realize what was happening. Some lycans can appear lucid even after the madness takes them. But Prince Einar blacks out. On one occasion, he killed a servant and dragged the body back to his quarters. Other servants found the decomposing corpse a few weeks later."

My gasp was loud in the bedroom. I pressed trembling fingers to my lips.

"That was ninety years ago," Arlo said. "Prince Einar has never killed in cold blood again. Even so, memories in the supernatural world are long. Many believe King Cyrus made a mistake by permitting Prince Einar to live. If he were anyone else, Cyrus would have killed him."

My heart pounded painfully. I couldn't deny what I'd seen downstairs. But I also couldn't dismiss the Einar who flirted with me over dinner and took me hiking. "Einar shelters supernaturals who need help," I said. "He built the maze to keep them safe."

"Yes," Arlo said, sadness heavy in his voice. "Einar has a good heart. And he knows what it is to be an outcast. He understands how it feels to lose everything. But lycans who can't control their beasts are dangerous. Prince Einar knows that too. He didn't build the maze to keep the people of Draithmere safe from the outside world. The grounds are secure enough for that." Arlo drew a deep breath. "Prince Einar built the maze to keep his people safe from him."

My breath hitched. My interactions with Einar ran through my mind like a movie strip, beginning with my father's office and ending with him clawing my arm downstairs.

"You left me alone with him," I said, anger kindling. "You took the night off—"

"I'm always a shout away. And Adina's potion has kept the prince's beast in check for decades. It's not foolproof, but it allows him to live a somewhat normal life."

Puzzle pieces fell into place. "The flasks," I said. "He drinks from them to control his animal side?"

Arlo nodded. "Adina is the most accomplished potion master in the world. She takes risks others won't. With a lot of experimentation, she's been able to craft mixtures that allow Prince Einar to shift normally, making the full transformation from man to beast. That's how your father was able to capture him on film. But the potion doesn't work all the time, and the effects wear off eventually." Arlo hesitated. "Adina thought perhaps..."

"Perhaps what?" I asked.

Arlo exhaled heavily. "The prince was taken with you from the moment he saw your photo. His attraction was obvious to all of us, and the two of you seemed drawn to each other despite your best efforts to stay apart. Adina theorized that love might help Prince Einar regain control of his beast. Fated mates are rare among lycans, but the histories tell of such matches occurring."

My body went hot, then cold. An odd lump formed in my throat. "Einar doesn't love me." He'd never said it. And why would he? The moments we'd shared had been engineered by others.

"I shouldn't have listened to Adina," Arlo said softly, his tone at odds with his fierce appearance. "Witches can be fanciful. None of us meant to hurt you, but I fear that's exactly what we've done."

"By feeding me spiked tea and throwing me into Einar's path?" I asked, bitterness welling. Arlo and I had laughed together. He'd treated me like a friend, not an experiment.

Arlo's face fell. He stepped toward me, one claw-tipped hand extended. "You should let me look at your arm."

I moved backward. "I said it's fine. And you said you need to see to Einar. You should go do that."

Silence fell. After a second, Arlo lowered his hand. "I'm sorry, Miss Ward. I know my words are meaningless at the moment. But I do mean them, and I hope you can forgive me for the part I played in this." He went to the door and opened it. Pausing on the threshold, he looked at me over his shoulder. For a moment, I thought he'd say more. But with a final look of regret, he left.

I counted to ten in my head. Then I rushed across the room and tried the door knob.

Locked.

As I'd suspected, Arlo had ways of making sure I didn't leave my room. Cursing under my breath, I hiked my sleeve up and examined my arm. Three slashes marred my forearm, the wounds red and ugly. Blood clotted in the furrows as my body struggled to heal.

My gaze drifted to the bed, a vision of Einar with his first aid kit filling my mind. Had *everything* been fake? Had any of our moments together meant anything at all? Or had it all been farce? A test trial fueled by Adina's potion, every interaction carried out under Arlo's watchful eye.

My chest tightened. Only vaguely aware of what I was doing, I went to the bathroom and started straightening the toiletries lined up on the sink. A therapist once told me that repetitive behaviors were rooted in an anxiety sufferer's need to regain control. I understood the theory well enough, but understanding *why* I did compulsive things didn't make me stop doing them. My anxiety was just part of me, like my hair color or the freckles I'd hated as a kid. I managed my disorder with medication because I refused to let it rule me.

My fingers brushed my prescription. The bottle tipped, rolled, and clattered to the floor.

Memories of Einar rose, his silver gaze steady as he nodded toward the bottle protruding from my pocket. *"There's no shame in taking medicine. An ailment in the mind is the same as an ailment in the body. Treating anxiety is no different than setting a broken bone. You'll receive no judgment from me."*

My heart sped up. *"You'll receive no judgment from me."*

But I'd judged him. Was his ailment all that different from mine? He lost control, but he managed his condition as best as he could. And the second I'd learned of it, I was prepared to write him off as a lost cause.

I bent and retrieved the bottle from the floor.

"You're under my skin, Harper Ward. And the harder I try to fight it, the more I want to make you mine. No one challenges me like you do. No one dares. Every time we argue, I walk away wondering if I should have kissed you instead."

He'd shopped for me. Lined up labels for me. Because he understood how it felt to lose control. I couldn't give up on him.

"Arlo?" I called, rushing from the bathroom.

Goliath popped into existence directly in front of me, his body wreathed in a cloud of black smoke.

I stumbled backward, and I coughed as smoke filled my lungs. "What—?"

"Shh," Goliath said, stepping from the cloud. His face was pale under his tattoos, and his tail curled tightly around his hip. "We have to be quiet," he said, his voice barely above a whisper. "Arlo won't be gone long. If you want to see Einar, we've got like five minutes to get you downstairs."

My heart skipped a beat. "I *do* want to see him."

Goliath offered a shaky smile. "I thought you might say that." He sobered. "Harper... I never wanted to lie to you. But Prince Einar's story is his to tell."

Doubt crept in. "Well, he never told it. Not to me."

"Because he was afraid to drive you away." Determination filled Goliath's eyes. "None of us have ever seen him like this. He's happy with you. Adina has spent decades searching for a cure. And then you arrived. Maybe you're the cure, Harper. Fate is powerful magic."

Hope soared in my chest. "What do I have to do?"

"Just be you. Arlo is probably still in the crypt where Einar stays when he's in one of his rages. If I can get you to the trap door, you can enter and try to break through to Einar. Arlo might balk at first, but he'll keep you safe."

I nodded. Then my heart sank. "Arlo locked me in."

Goliath scoffed. "Locks can't hold me." He put out his hand. "Hang on tight. This will feel weird."

I gripped his hand. And the floor dropped from under me. A scream lodged in my throat as I plummeted, the world dissolving into smoke. A second later, my feet slammed into a hard surface, buckling my knees.

I sagged to the ground, coughing as I tried to catch my breath.

"Sorry," Goliath whispered, bending over me. "There's no good way to prepare someone for morphing."

I nodded, one hand pressed to the paved path that connected the garage to the main house. Evening air swirled around me, ferrying away the last of the smoke. Ahead, a door leading into the garage stood ajar.

"It's through there," Goliath said in a low voice.

I let him tug me to my feet. Together, we entered the darkened garage. Moonlight streamed through windows set high on the walls. Several vehicles filled the space, chrome gleaming in the gloom.

And Arlo lay crumpled on his side next to a flat door built into the concrete floor. His eyes were closed, his mouth slack. Blood trickled from a cut on his forehead.

Just as I drew breath to scream, a hand clamped over my mouth. An arm wrapped around my waist, hauling me onto my tiptoes. "Quiet, *chère*," a masculine, French-accented voice breathed in my ear. "We don't want to wake our sleeping friend." In my peripheral vision, a second man whipped a black hood over Goliath's head. When Goliath struggled, the man spun him around and buried his fist in Goliath's stomach. Goliath crumpled with a pained wheeze.

My captor tightened his arm around my midsection, cutting off my breath before I could attempt to protest. "Someone open that fucking trap door!" His lips caressed my ear, and my skin crawled as his breath fluttered over my neck. "We're going to see how well your boyfriend fights when he doesn't have his drugs to help him."

Half a dozen wolves sprang from the shadows, their fangs bared and their eyes gleaming like gold coins in the darkened garage.

Werewolves. They were smaller than Einar in his lycan form.

A third man dressed in head-to-toe black strode from between two cars. He carried a pistol, and the hilt of an honest-to-goodness broadsword poked over his shoulder. As he approached the trap door, a giant crow swooped out of nowhere, its talons aimed directly at the man's head.

He ducked, cursing.

"Help him, Hector!" the man holding me shouted. The man who punched Goliath darted forward. He waved his arms, shouting as he attempted to scare off the crow.

Screeching, the crow wheeled in the air, its wings spread wide. As it swooped toward the ground, it shifted in a flurry of black feathers. A beat later, Myrna stepped to the ground on two legs. Her white dress fluttered around her ankles as she moved in front of Arlo and the trap door.

"Stop right there!" the man with the pistol shouted. He leveled the gun at Myrna. "Not another step closer."

The werewolves on four legs bared their fangs.

Myrna paid them no attention. She stared at the man holding me, her eyes wide and red-rimmed. Slowly, she lifted a finger and pointed at him.

"I've seen your death, Armand Reverdin!" she cried. "You will burn in the inferno, your flesh melting from your bones!"

My captor tensed. His arm around my waist tightened like

a band of iron, threatening to crush my ribs. Next to me, Goliath slumped on his knees, his head sagging under the hood.

The wolves didn't move. A few cast wary looks at my captor, who was apparently called Armand.

Myrna kept her finger outstretched. An eerie wind tugged at her dress, making the fabric whip around her legs.

Tension filled the garage. A few of the werewolves in beast form slunk backward. The man with the pistol looked at Armand. "Should we...seize her?"

"Kill her," Armand snarled.

Distant shouts drifted from somewhere behind me. Armand whirled, dragging me with him. The door flew open with a metallic shriek, and another man stumbled into the garage.

"They're coming, sir!" he gasped, his face leached of color. "There's some kind of fucked-up hedge maze in the back. People are pouring from it. Rothkilde has an army!"

The shouts from outside grew louder. The thunder of hooves followed. My heart leapt. The centaurs and the others were coming.

Armand swung back around, his palm tight over my mouth. His chest lifted against my back, and I got the sense he grappled with his next steps as he realized he was in danger of being trapped. "Intercept them!" he yelled finally. "We'll have to fight our way out."

The werewolves on four legs growled and then shot past us. My elation evaporated, and worry gripped me as I imagined them clashing with Leander and the others from the maze. On the ground, Arlo stirred, his eyelids fluttering. Relief coursed through me even as I mentally pleaded with him to stay still. If he tried to fight, I had no doubt Armand would kill him.

"Bring the demon!" Armand barked. Hector scrambled to obey.

Myrna caught my eye. I couldn't be certain, but I thought she gave me a subtle nod. Then she shifted in a blur, reforming into a crow and zooming toward the rafters.

The man with the pistol aimed it toward the ceiling.

"Don't shoot, you idiot!" Armand yelled. "The bullets will ricochet."

Outside, a wolf gave a high-pitched yelp. The shouts grew louder. Hector and the man with the pistol lifted Arlo from the ground. They were both big men, but they clearly struggled under Arlo's weight.

"Leave the runt," Armand ordered. "He's not worth the hassle." Just as I realized he spoke of Goliath, something hard struck my head. Pain exploded in my skull.

And everything went black.

CHAPTER TWENTY

HARPER

I opened my eyes, and everything was gray. An unpleasant odor hung in the air, like cheap cleaner mixed with mold. As my eyes adjusted, I took stock of my surroundings.

I lay on my side on a surface so hard it had to be concrete. Damp seeped into my clothes, which were thankfully still on my body. I had no reason to think Armand had designs on me, but self-preservation meant assuming everything was on the table.

The pain in my forearm had faded to a dull ache. The pain in the back of my skull was a bright, shiny beacon of *mother-fucking ow*. I squeezed my eyes shut as I took shallow breaths, willing away my sudden nausea. Wherever I was, it wasn't good. Puking would make everything worse.

"Harper?"

My eyes flew open. Adrenaline pumped through my veins, and I sat up and turned toward the sound of my father's voice. Dizziness slammed into me, followed by another wave of nausea. My head throbbed, and I groaned as I leaned forward, saliva flooding my mouth.

"Harper!" Shoes shuffled on concrete, and then my father knelt next to me. His hand shook as he touched my shoulder, and his voice was low and hoarse. "Oh god, what have they done to you?"

The pain and nausea receded enough for me to lift my head. My eyes focused enough for me to make out the windowless concrete cell around us. No bars, though. Just a big metal door painted the same dingy gray. An open toilet stood against one wall. There was nothing else. Just concrete.

And my father.

"What are you doing here?" I asked. He looked terrible, his jaw covered in what appeared to be several days' worth of white stubble. His hair stuck up in greasy spikes, and he'd lost his glasses. A yellowish stain ringed his neckline where he'd obviously sweat.

Dad's face crumpled. "I'm so sorry," he said. "I was only trying to help. The gauze came in the mail, and I didn't know what to do, so I went to the Sound. I never should have let you go with Rothkilde. Your mother always said my pride was going to eclipse my talent, and she was right." He gave a short, broken sob. "Maggie was always right. She was so smart...so good, she—"

"Dad," I said, cutting off his babbling. I gripped his shoulders and tried to ignore the way the movement made a fresh spike of pain stab the back of my head. "What do you mean about gauze? What came in the mail? Give me the facts as they happened."

Those were the magic words. My father's gaze sharpened, and he drew a shuddering breath. "A couple days after you left, Rothkilde sent bloodied gauze to the house, along with a note letting me know I could expect worse if I didn't turn over all the footage of his shift."

My breath froze in my lungs. In my mind's eye, Einar bent

over my foot, his long, elegant fingers skillfully wrapping gauze around my toe. He'd tended my injury—and then shipped the bloodied aftermath to my father.

"I was terrified," Dad said, "and I was so ashamed. The footage wasn't important anymore. My only priority was getting you out of Rothkilde's house." A hard edge entered my father's voice. "Contrary to what he might think, I don't have contacts in the supernatural world. I didn't know where to turn, so I returned to the place where everything started."

"You went back to the Puget Sound," I said.

Dad nodded, his eyes filling with tears. "I took a tent and made camp near the spot where I saw Rothkilde shift. The first night, nothing happened. But the second night, the werewolves found me. They promised to help if I gave them the gauze. They said Rothkilde was a horrible man, and they could track you through your blood. The second I handed it over, they beat me and then brought me here." My father ran his bloodshot gaze over my face. "Did they hurt you?"

I reached up and probed the back of my scalp. A knot rose from the center of my skull, but my hair was dry, and I didn't feel any open wounds. "I think I'm okay," I said. "How long have I been here?"

"A few hours." My father's expression turned grave. "Harper, listen to me. Whatever happens, cooperate as much as you can. Armand is more dangerous than you think."

"Sage advice," Armand said through the door. It swung open with a loud squeal, and he entered with Hector behind him. Armand smiled at me. The expression didn't reach his icy blue eyes. "You should listen to your father, *chère*."

Dad stood. His voice trembled, but he looked Armand in the eye as he spoke. "Harper hasn't done anything wrong, Mr. Reverdin. She's innocent in all of this."

"Hector," Armand said softly.

Hector moved around him, gripped my father by the throat, and flung him against the wall.

A scream ripped from me as I surged to my feet. Hector delivered a brutal kick to my father's stomach. I screamed again as Armand gripped my upper arm and dragged me from the cell.

"Please!" I pleaded. "Don't hurt him!"

"That's up to you," Armand said, manhandling me into what appeared to be a massive warehouse. Giant metal shelving soared toward the ceiling that had to be forty feet high. Stone statuary and plastic fencing materials lined the shelves, but even at a distance, I could see that everything was coated in dust. Wherever Armand had brought me, it wasn't an active business.

I struggled to stay on my feet as he strode down a broad aisle, his fingers biting into my bicep. We rounded the end of a row of shelves, and my heart plummeted at the sight of Arlo tied to a metal chair. He was in human form, and his face was a black-and-blue mess. One eye was half swollen shut. Blood ran freely from a cut on his cheekbone. His arms were secured behind his back. A rope ran around his chest, binding him to the chair.

Four men with gold-sheened eyes stood in a half circle behind him. One broke from the group, grabbed a second metal chair from behind a stack of wooden pallets, and set it down. He grinned at me as he stepped back and bowed.

"A throne fit for a princess," he said, mockery in his tone.

"More like a whore," Hector said, striding from behind Armand. "She spread her legs for Rothkilde easily enough. I can smell the lycan stench from here."

Armand shoved me into the chair so hard it skidded on the concrete and started to tip. The first man caught me and slammed the chair onto all four legs so hard my teeth clicked together.

"There you go, princess," he said, smoothing my hair off my shoulder.

"Don't fucking touch me!" I growled, jerking away. The men laughed.

Arlo made a soft sound. When I looked at him, warning gleamed in his dark eyes.

Armand caught the silent communication. "Your friend?" he asked me, gesturing to Arlo. "That was a mistake on your part, human. A Legerdemain demon will slit his own mother's throat for enough coin."

I clamped my mouth shut, hatred searing my insides. At the same time, confusion coursed through me. Arlo was just sitting there. He was bound, yes, but he was also capable of pulling weapons out of thin air and locking doors with magic. Why wasn't he fighting back?

"They're all thieves and assassins," Armand said. He went to Arlo and kicked the front leg of Arlo's chair, knocking it so Arlo faced me. Then he circled the chair and yanked Arlo's head back. "Duplicity is baked into their bones. But they're powerful. I'll give them that." Armand's lips curved, his blue eyes cold and flat as he looked at me. "However, the Legerdemain have one glaring weakness. Tie their arms behind their back, and they can't perform any of their party tricks. If you want to nullify their magic permanently, it's as easy as chopping their hands off."

"Don't!" I cried before I could stop myself. My heart pounded, sending fresh blasts of pain through the knot on my head.

Armand chuckled as he released Arlo's hair. "*Non*. Not right now, anyway. I have other business to attend to."

Footsteps rang out. A man with long, curved horns

appeared around the end of a row of metal shelves. Shirtless, he wore a pair of light brown leather pants slung low on his hips. Several beaded necklaces descended to the center of his chest. He was obviously a demon, but his horns were the color of bone, and his features were reptilian. As he neared, I realized the beads on his necklaces were teeth.

My nausea came roaring back. It intensified as I got a better look at his pants. A faded anchor with a rose wrapped around it was inked onto one of his thighs. Because the pants weren't animal skin. They were human skin.

"Some of that business better be mine," the demon called out. As he passed Arlo's chair, Arlo caught sight of him and stiffened.

Armand narrowed his eyes.

The demon's necklaces clinked softly as he stopped before Armand. "I did my part, Reverdin. Now give me my money so I can be on my way."

Armand's eyes grew colder. "Not yet, Urzeb. Three of my wolves are unaccounted for. They were excellent fighters. I want them back. I need a bloodhound."

Urzeb snarled, displaying curved fangs. When he spoke, a forked tongue flashed in his mouth. "That name is offensive to my people. If you want to find your wolves, find them yourself. I tracked the human female and led you to Draithmere. That was our agreement."

Tension vibrated in the space between Armand and the demon. My scalp prickled, and my mouth went dry as I held my breath. In the corner of my vision, Hector and one of the other werewolves eased forward.

Urzeb's nostrils flared. He kept his gaze pinned on Armand, but there was no question he was aware of the wolves closing in on him.

"If you kill me, Reverdin," he said softly, "you'll die screaming on a Scorab table as my kin dine on your flesh."

The air itself seemed to hold its breath. I waited, my heart racing, prepared for violence to break out.

Finally, Armand snapped his fingers. "Fine. You'll have your payment." As Hector moved forward and placed a velvet bag in his hand, Armand glowered at Urzeb. "But don't expect to do business with me again."

"I wouldn't dream of it," Urzeb said. He tested the bag's weight in his palm, then withdrew a gold coin and examined it. Apparently satisfied, he replaced the coin and then turned to Arlo. "Should I give my regards to the Legerdemain when I return to Durzu? I can pass a message along if you like."

Arlo glared at him. Ghostly horns flickered around his head.

Urzeb laughed. "Nothing to say, princeling? I suppose you're not allowed to speak unless Rothkilde gives his permission." He tossed the bag of coins into the air and then caught it. "Being a lycan's lapdog must pay well."

Menace glittered in Arlo's eyes. "You and I will meet again one day. I vow it. And your bones will litter the plains of Durzu."

Urzeb smirked, but something like wariness flitted through his eyes, the emotion there and gone so quickly I couldn't be certain I'd seen it.

"Doubtful," he told Arlo. "You've always been a disgrace. Unworthy of your father's name. Perhaps that's why you hide on this plane with the stink of humans clogging your nose." Urzeb turned back to Armand and swept a mocking bow. "It's been a pleasure, Reverdin." Straightening, he disappeared.

For a moment, Armand was still and silent, his gaze on the spot where Urzeb had stood. "Put her on her stomach," he said finally.

Hands seized me. Fear exploded in my chest as I was shoved face down on the concrete.

"No!" Arlo shouted. "Don't!—" His voice ended in a grunt as the sound of flesh striking flesh echoed through the warehouse.

The men held me down. My breath came in gasps as I turned my head, my cheek pressed to the concrete. "What are you doing?" I asked, my voice high-pitched and foreign in my ears.

"Hold her arm out to the side," Armand ordered.

I fought but it was useless. Hector gripped my elbow and straightened my arm. Another man stepped on my forearm, his boot digging into Einar's claw marks hidden under my sweater. Pain lashed me, and I couldn't hold back my scream.

"Now, now," Armand said, crouching next to my head. A knife glinted in his hand. "You're getting ahead of yourself, *chère*. You should save your strength. And your cries." He pushed my hair off my forehead. "I assure you, the worst is yet to come."

I panted, fear clawing at my guts. The knife filled my vision. "Please, don't do this," I begged.

"I don't have a choice," Armand said. His tone turned polite, almost reasonable. "Draithmere is spelled. Only its inhabitants can find it. But your father was kind enough to give me a sample of your blood, which allowed me to hire Urzeb to track you." Armand flipped the knife once, the hilt slapping into his palm. "Scorab demons can find anyone with even the smallest drop of blood. It's a pity they're such assholes, *non*?"

My heart pounded against the concrete. My mouth was so dry that my tongue stuck to the inside of my cheek.

Armand sighed. "I admit, the loss of my wolves irks me. But I can face Rothkilde without them. Now that he doesn't have his Legerdemain handler, he's vulnerable. And when he's vulnerable, he can be killed. I just need a powerful enough motivator to make him break the chains of his prison. That's where you come in."

Fear choked me. Tears and sweat stung my eyes.

Hector stepped on my wrist.

Armand smiled.

Then he sliced my pinky off.

CHAPTER TWENTY-ONE

EINAR

Consciousness returned like floodlights filling a pitch-black room. I lay on my side with the familiar cool, dry air of the crypt in my nostrils.

Harper.

I jumped to my feet, expecting to hear the clatter of my chains against the concrete. But I was unbound.

"Prince Einar!" Goliath stepped from the shadows with Adina at his heels. Signs of fatigue clung to both of them, their clothes rumpled and their eyes sunken.

"How long have I been out?" I demanded, panic rising. "Where's Arlo? Why didn't he chain me? Is Harper safe?"

"Armand Reverdin took her," Goliath said, his tail tucked between his legs. "He got Arlo, too. He would have taken me, but Myrna distracted him."

Red descended over my vision. If I hadn't just emerged from an episode of madness, I would have immediately spiraled again. Even so, my beast threatened to snap its restraints.

"When?" I rasped.

"Two days ago," Adina said.

Armand had Harper. He fucking had her. *Werewolves* had entered Draithmere and taken the only woman I ever...

I tried to smother the thought, but it broke through anyway, the force of my realization almost taking me to my knees.

I loved her. Harper was the only woman I'd ever loved. And I'd failed to protect her because I was weak. Broken.

"Your Highness?" Goliath ventured. He and Adina stared at me, a mixture of wariness and expectation on their faces.

I stalked to the ladder built into the side of the crypt. "Tell me everything," I barked over my shoulder. "Leave nothing out."

By the time I entered my study, Goliath and Adina had filled me in on the attack. No one knew how Armand had entered Draithmere. But it didn't matter. Somehow, he'd breached the boundaries. Forty-eight hours later, Harper and Arlo were missing, and I had no fucking clue how to find them. And without Arlo, I couldn't search for them. I was trapped at Draithmere.

Fire licked through my veins as I went to my desk and pulled out a flask.

"It's a fresh brew," Adina said, watching me carefully. "I made it stronger this time."

I grunted my acknowledgment. But it didn't matter. The brew might keep the madness at bay, but what good was lucidity when I couldn't find Harper? The brew splashed into my empty stomach. When I'd drained the flask, I tossed it across the study. It smashed into the wall, embedding itself into wood paneling that had graced the room since the turn of the previous century.

Goliath gasped. Adina stepped forward, her hands raised in a soothing gesture.

"Your Highness, we have to stay calm."

I looked around for something else to throw.

Classical music drifted from my desk. Frowning, I stepped back and looked down. The muffled noise continued, the musical scales rising and falling. I opened the top drawer and pulled out a mobile phone.

Harper's phone, which I'd taken from her the night I brought her to Draithmere. Arlo must have lifted the muffling spell. Orson Ward's face filled the screen. The word "DAD" appeared above his photo.

I swiped the screen and put the phone to my ear. "Rothkilde."

"Oh, thank god," Orson gasped. A blunt sound vibrated across the line, and he gave a muffled cry. "All right, all right!"

Goliath and Adina moved to the edge of my desk.

"Ward?" I demanded. "Where are you?"

He spoke in a breathless rush. "I know where Harper is. That's all I can say." He rattled off an address, and I tucked the phone between my ear and shoulder and scribbled it on the first piece of paper I could find.

"Is Harper with you?" I asked, gripping the phone more tightly.

The call ended.

I pulled the phone away from my ear. Orson was gone.

"Google the address," Adina said, but I was already typing. The result that popped up on the screen made me frown.

"This looks like a gas station," I said. "It's about ten miles away." But it might as well have been ten thousand. Without Arlo, I couldn't venture beyond Draithmere's boundaries.

"I'll go," Goliath said.

I shook my head. "I can't ask that of you. This is almost definitely a trap." Armand didn't want to meet for a quick chat. He was probably lying in wait with his entire pack ready to pounce. I'd underestimated him. As a new alpha, he wanted to cement his power. He'd broken into Draithmere, probably hoping to kill me. Instead, he'd taken Arlo and Harper. Now, he wanted another shot at me—and anyone else he could kill in the process.

Goliath's chin went up. "Harper is my friend. Respectfully, Prince Einar, you don't have to ask. I'm going."

"Me too," Adina said. "I owe it to Harper to make sure she gets home safely."

Home. Harper almost certainly didn't think of Draithmere as her home. But the house felt more like one with her in it.

"I can pull one person with me when I morph," Goliath said. "If we can get Keir to help, he could bring someone too. That'll make four of us against Armand and his pack."

The odds were terrible, especially with four residents of the maze going up against the Puget Sound werewolves. Adina was powerful, but she was no warrior. Her magic was potion-based. Keir was prone to fainting. Goliath's dragon was dormant.

On the other hand, if Harper was out there, I had to try.

"Let's talk to Keir," I said.

~

Ten minutes later, I watched Keir link arms with Leander. We stood at the maze's entrance under a twilight sky, and all my instincts told me this rescue mission was a terrible, very bad idea.

A short distance away, Goliath and Adina held hands, prepared to morph to the address Orson had given me. It was clear *someone* had forced him to make that phone call. Armand must have gotten to him. Did that mean Orson was working with the werewolves against his own daughter? I didn't want to believe it, but I had to assume the worst.

"We're ready," Goliath said.

I looked at Keir and Leander. "Are you two absolutely certain you're on board with this? You're not battle-tested. There's zero shame in staying behind."

Leander's amethyst eyes glinted with determination. He'd pulled his hair into a top knot, and feathers poked from the red mass like a spiky crown. "I may not be a warrior, my prince, but I am very difficult to kill."

Keir inclined his head in my direction. "I'm the first to admit I'm a poor fighter, Your Highness, but I can offer transport. You've helped all of us through the years. Now let us help you."

Gratitude swelled my chest. I met each of their gazes as I spoke. "I admire your bravery. It takes courage to enter enemy territory like this. You're doing what I can't, and you have my sincere thanks. Please be careful."

"We will," Goliath said. He looked at Keir. "You remember the plan? We go in fast, grab Harper if she's there, and poof out. No lingering."

Keir nodded. "No lingering."

"Right, then. On three..." Goliath counted down, and he and Adina winked out of sight. A split second later, Keir disappeared with Leander.

Minutes passed. I waited, a mix of pride, nerves, and guilt swirling through me. My people—no, my *friends*—had stepped up when I needed them. But my weakness was responsible for Armand's attack in the first place. If I hadn't lost control, he would have never been able to ambush Arlo and kidnap Harper. And my failure extended even farther back. I'd taken Harper from her home—and put her in Armand's path.

Everything was my fault. And what was I doing to fix the mess I'd made? Waiting on the lawn like a coward while the people who depended on me for safety put their lives on the line for—

Goliath and Adina appeared in a cloud of smoke. A beat later, Keir popped into existence with Leander in tow. Keir swayed on his feet, his forehead beaded with sweat.

"Easy," Leander said, thrusting a shoulder under Keir's armpit. Keir's eyelids fluttered, and he groaned as the phoenix propped him up.

"What happened?" I asked, going to Goliath.

His face was devoid of color, the dragon scales on his cheeks faded to a sickly green. He held something—a bundle wrapped in what appeared to be a white cloth napkin.

Between one breath and the next, I gripped his shirt in two fists and hauled him off the ground. "Tell me what happened!" I growled, the fire within me flaring to life.

Goliath's mouth worked as he clearly struggled to speak. The bundle slipped from his hand and fell to the ground. An object rolled across the grass and into a patch of moonlight. The silvery glow threw the napkin's contents into stark relief.

I stared, my mind refusing to comprehend what I was seeing.

But I knew. I knew.

Harper's little finger. Severed at the second knuckle. The nail carefully shaped and coated with a layer of the palest pink.

Goliath spoke in a trembling voice. "The gas station was abandoned. We found the..." He gulped. "We found th-that and a note." He pulled a piece of paper from his pocket. "Armand gives an address. He demands you meet him in person tonight, or he'll..." Goliath's voice faltered. He shook his head.

"Or what?" I asked, rage building.

Goliath drew a deep breath. "Or he'll continue sending pieces."

Black smeared my vision. The fire followed. It pumped through my veins as the scenery around me rippled. My fangs shot down, shredding my bottom lip. Gasps rang out. Around me, people cringed away, their faces suddenly too blurry to make out.

Helpless. I was utterly helpless, trapped in my prison. Armand might as well have been holding Harper on the moon. I couldn't participate in his twisted scavenger hunt. Because I couldn't fucking get to her.

"Einar Rothkilde!" a woman called, her voice cutting through the tempest in my mind.

I swung toward the sound in time to see Myrna emerge from the maze. Her beauty was flawless, and her white gown was immaculate as she came to me. Rising on tiptoe, she cupped cool hands around my jaw.

"Listen to me, prince of lycans." Myrna's words overlapped as if she spoke from a great distance. "The gods gifted and cursed me to see the deaths of those around me. My solace is that I only see one death at a time. I've seen Armand Reverdin's demise."

"What does that mean?" I croaked, the last threads of my sanity threatening to unravel.

"Armand Reverdin is fated to die before you or anyone else from Draithmere." Myrna dropped her hands from my face and stepped back. Her eyes grew unfocused. "Death hovers just over Reverdin's shoulder. He won't survive this night."

I stared at Myrna, the faintest hope stirring in my chest. As swiftly as the emotion arrived, it succumbed to frustration. "I believe you, but I don't see how I can face him. Without Arlo's magic, I'm trapped at Draithmere."

Adina stepped forward. "You don't have Arlo's magic, but

you have us." She looked around those assembled on the lawn. "If we combine our efforts, we might be strong enough to bend the boundaries long enough for you to slip through."

Leander nodded. "Yes. I've read of such things. Draithmere's boundaries were raised with magic. Maybe magic can bring them down."

"I'm in," Goliath said. His fangs flashed as he grimaced. "Whatever it takes to finish those Puget Sound fuckers for good, I'm all for it."

The hedges rustled, and then Rolfe emerged in human form. He towered above the rest of the group as he spoke in a soft rumble. "I'd like to help, too. You gave me a home, Prince Einar. My magic is yours for as long as you need it."

"Mine as well," a centaur said, striding from the maze with a sword strapped to his back. His tail swished, and his expression was forbidding as he stopped at the edge of the crowd. "I refuse to cower in fear while two of our own are threatened. I will fight."

"As will I," Keir said. The vampire was pale, but he stood tall, his shoulders thrown back. "The werewolves hurt people we love." Keir looked at Goliath. "What was that phrase you taught me? Fuck around and...?"

"Find out," Goliath said, a smile spreading across his face. He turned to me. "Reverdin fucked around. It's time for him to find out how stupid that was."

The hedges shivered again, and more people emerged from the maze. Sirens and ogres. A pair of mermen with fish scale clothing and glittering tridents. Several jaguar shifters with deep amber eyes. One by one, the residents of the maze offered their magic. The lawn filled with supernaturals. Power hummed in the air.

Adina came to my side, a look of wonder on her face as she surveyed the crowd.

"Do you think this can work?" I asked her under my breath.

She turned to me. "Some of us are weaker than others. A few of us are broken. But together, our magic is strong."

Hope tried to rise again. This time, I let it.

"All right," I said, looking around at my people. I lifted my voice. "Let's go knock down that barrier!"

Cheers went up, along with a few battle cries. We left the maze behind and rushed through the night, arriving at the first barrier in under ten minutes. Magic prickled against my skin, the stinging sensation like static electricity on steroids. It was nothing compared to what Harper had endured. Was probably still enduring.

Fresh anger surged, but I forced it down. If I wanted Harper back, I had to keep control.

"Line up!" I shouted. Draithmere's lights shone in the distance. Trees rose around us. Out in the open, the maze's inhabitants seemed fewer. Not much of an army at all.

But they were all I had—and I *had* to try.

"Everyone join hands!" Adina called, taking mine. Goliath appeared on my other side.

"So..." he said, "should we just rush it?"

"That's not a bad idea," Adina said. "Magic is grounded in intention. And the barrier is metaphysical."

"Yeah, you're going to need to explain that to me like I'm five."

Adina adopted a patient tone. "If we merely envision ourselves tearing it down, we might not make it happen. But if we run at it, we're putting actions to words."

Goliath flicked his tail behind him. "Let's do it. You ready, Your Highness?"

"Yes," I said, sweat trickling down my back. My heart raced. I had no idea what would happen if the barrier held. It might injure me. Or kill me.

"For Arlo," Goliath murmured.

Adina squeezed my hand.

"For Harper," I said, squeezing back. Looking down one side of the line, then the other, I raised my voice. "We're going to crush this thing! Then we're going to find Armand Reverdin and deliver the death Myrna promised him!"

Roars split the air. The ground shook as hooves and talons clawed at the earth. Power swelled, lifting the hair on my nape.

I'm coming, Harper.

"Now!" I bellowed. Hand in hand with my people, I charged the barrier that had imprisoned me for ninety years. As we ran, light arced before us, magic surging like a tidal wave. Energy crackled. Fuck me, we were doing it. I leaned forward, a vision of Harper in my head.

The wave slammed into an invisible wall, the force of the impact throwing me backward. Goliath and Adina fell to the ground, their hands slipping from mine. I staggered but managed to stay on my feet as the wave of magic sloshed up the wall and spread outward, lightning forking around its edges.

For a moment, everything was still. Nothing happened. Doubt gnawed at the edges of my mind. Around me, people stood on shaky legs, their gazes trained on the barrier.

The lightning winked out, plunging the forest around us into darkness. I clenched my jaw, doubt settling into anger.

"Look!" someone cried.

Light flashed high on the wall. Then it spread, forming a crack. More cracks formed. They spiderwebbed across the transparent barrier, forking and growing wider. Wider. The web stretched across the air, spreading and spreading and lighting up the forest around us.

BOOM.

A rush of air knocked me backward. For a moment, the sky lit up, the night turning to day.

The barrier dropped, a million fragments of light shimmering in the air before disappearing. Moments later, another boom echoed in the distance...then another. All three barriers had fallen. I was free.

For a second, silence reigned. Then everyone broke into a thunderous cheer. Leander and Keir embraced, pounding each other on the back. Rolfe gazed up at the last of the disintegrating fragments with a soft smile on his face. Triumph pumped hot in my veins as I looked at a jubilant Goliath.

"You got that address?"

His eyes flashed. The dragon scales on his face glittered like emeralds. "I absolutely do."

CHAPTER TWENTY-TWO

HARPER

Food paraded in a steady stream behind my closed lids. Chicken. Pasta. Baskets of fresh bread glistening with butter glaze.

It was stupid to indulge myself this way. But I couldn't help it. Every time I closed my eyes now, food dominated my dreams. I'd given up wishing for freedom. Or dignity. Or even uninterrupted sleep.

No, I just wanted a bowl of mashed potatoes and a Diet Coke. My mouth watered, the hiss of carbonation sizzling in my ears. God, Diet Coke—

"Harper?"

I opened my eyes, meeting my father's gaze across the cell. He sat against the wall, his knees drawn to his chest in a pose that matched mine. I didn't need a mirror to know our appearances matched too. The sweat stains on his shirt were darker than when I first saw him. His hair didn't stick up anymore. Now, it lay flat and slick against his scalp.

"Yeah?" I asked, my voice rusty.

Dad's throat worked as he swallowed. "Are you in pain?"

I tucked my right hand behind my left, hiding the dirty, blood-encrusted bandage Hector had tied around my pinky. "I'm okay," I lied. "It doesn't hurt anymore."

My father nodded slowly, but his expression told me he didn't believe me. We hadn't spoken much since Armand shoved us back in the cell. We both knew our conversations weren't private.

And it wasn't like we could hatch an escape plan. The metal door stayed shut except for the brief moments when someone thrust a bucket of water into the cell.

At first, I tried to mark time by how often the bucket appeared. But I couldn't figure out a pattern, and I had no idea how long Dad and I had been imprisoned. Two days? Four? Not a week, surely. Not yet. My hunger was still bearable.

But my hope for release was dwindling. Based on fragments of conversation that floated through the door, Armand was using me as bait to lure Einar into facing off with him in battle.

But Einar wasn't coming. Arlo's talk of fated mates was a distant memory.

My throat tightened. For all I knew, Arlo was dead. He'd gone wild after Armand took my finger, thrashing and screaming as he fought to break his bonds. Hector and the others subdued him, and the sound of fists thudding into flesh had followed me as Armand dragged me to the cell and dumped me inside.

"Strings," Dad said softly.

I startled, meeting his eyes. "You haven't called me that since I was little." The nickname was silly—the end result of him pretending he'd named me after all the instruments in an orchestra. He never got around to "harp," instead listing all the other options.

"No shoes in the house, Oboe."

"Daddy!" I'd protest. *"My name isn't oboe."*

"You're right. Put them on the shoe rack, Viola."

The game could last for hours, irritating my mother and making me laugh. Feigning defeat, my father would finally throw up his hands. *"Fine! You win. I named you Strings."*

Dad's smile was tired as he looked at me now. "It drove your mother nuts. I think I got all the way up to sixty instruments one time."

"She secretly liked it, though."

"Yeah. She did." My father stood. With a glance at the door, he crossed the cell and sat beside me.

I tensed, and I couldn't keep the tremor from my voice as I whispered, "They could come in."

"Let them," Dad said, putting an arm around me.

I rested my head on his shoulder, the weight of captivity easing slightly. We sat, wordless conversation passing between us. My father had been a journalist in war zones. He'd covered coups and civil unrest around the world. And while I didn't yet have my degree, I had enough journalistic training to understand the reality of our situation.

Armand didn't care if we talked. He wasn't worried about us scheming. And he didn't mind if we overheard him talking with his men. Because Armand didn't intend for my father and me to live. Our value as captives dwindled with every moment Einar failed to appear.

Eventually, our value would wilt to nothing. And Armand would kill us.

Dad tipped his head to the side, leaning it gently against mine. "Your mother always wanted more children," he said. "She was heartbroken when we couldn't give you a sibling. But then you grew, and we both realized we got it right on the first try. You're the best story we ever wrote."

Tears flooded my eyes. I drew a shaky breath. "I miss Mom a lot."

"Me too." He paused, and then tears filled his voice. "I've done so many things I'm not proud of. But I have never once failed to be proud of you. I love you, Harper, and when we get out of here, I'm going to do whatever I can to make you proud of me."

I lifted my head and looked at him. "I—"

A boom cut the air. The ground shuddered, and the fluorescent lights overhead flickered. Men's shouts rang out, followed by pounding footsteps.

Dad and I struggled to our feet. A second later, the door flew open, and a frazzled-looking Hector filled the doorway. Snarling, he lunged forward and seized my wrist.

"Hey!" my father yelled. "What's going on?"

Hector backhanded him, sending my father flying.

"Dad!" I reached for my father, but Hector gripped my arm and dragged me from the cell.

I stumbled along with him, lightheadedness swarming me. Another boom shook the building, making the lights flicker again. We entered the main part of the warehouse, where chaos reigned.

Men shouted as they ran down the aisles. A werewolf on four legs streaked past us, its fangs bared and its fur coated with dust. More dust clouded the air. As soon as Hector dragged me around a corner, I knew why. Dozens of statues lay shattered on the ground.

Armand's shouts echoed from somewhere. "They're hitting the doors! Everybody to the front!"

Booted footsteps rang out. Through the gaps in the shelving, I saw men sprinting to carry out his orders. My heart soared. Einar had come. He was here, and it sounded like he had serious backup.

BOOM. Another impact shook the warehouse. More statues crashed to the ground.

As Hector dragged me past the debris, Armand appeared from around the end of the aisle. His eyes glittered bright gold. The pistol in his hand sent a chill down my spine.

"Where's the demon?" he shouted at Hector.

Hector gripped my arm more tightly. "You told me to get the woman."

For a second, I thought Armand might shoot Hector. "You fucking idiot! If the demon gets loose, we're all dead."

BOOM. The world tilted, and I staggered sideways. Hector's fingers bit into my arm, keeping me upright as statues crashed around us. A scream tore from me, and I tried to duck, but he forced me into a run.

I stumbled along, half-blind as a series of pops filled the air. It took my sleep-deprived brain a second to recognize the sound of gunfire.

We rounded another corner, and Hector yanked me to a halt.

"Don't fucking move," he grated, disappearing behind a stack of pallets. Dust motes swirled, and he lifted a bound and dust-covered Arlo still secured to the metal chair. Blood seeped from a gash on Arlo's forehead, forming a river through the grime on his face. Joy coursed through me as he blinked open his eyes.

Hector stepped back, then pointed the gun at Arlo's head.

"No!" I screamed, terror rooting me to the floor.

Keir appeared out of nowhere next to Hector. The vampire took one look at the cut on Arlo's forehead and then swayed on his feet. Hector jumped, swinging the gun in Keir's direction. With a hiss, Keir moved in a blur, yanking Hector into him and plunging his fangs into Hector's throat.

Hector's gun went off. On a nearby shelf, the statue of a cupid exploded.

"Harper!" Arlo shouted, drawing my attention. "Undo my cuffs!"

Heart pumping, I raced around the pallets. Keir continued to feast on Hector, who sagged in the vampire's arms.

Basic metal handcuffs circled Arlo's wrists. "I don't have a key," I said.

"You don't need one. It doesn't take much at all to hold me as long as my arms are behind my back."

"You're kidding."

"No."

Huh. "Well, that sucks."

Arlo craned his head, giving me an exasperated look over his shoulder. "Nearly limitless power, one major design flaw. Trust me, if I ever find myself in front of the gods, I'll have a lot to say about it. In the meantime, can you get the freaking cuffs off me?"

"Oh, yes. Sorry." I fiddled with the cuffs, pressing the release catch. The metal fell away, and Arlo sprang into action, tearing the rope from his chest and jumping to his feet.

Hector's eyes rolled back in his head. His skin turned gray, and his jaw went slack. Keir wrenched his mouth from Hector's neck. Blood trickled from twin puncture wounds over Hector's jugular.

"Oh..." Keir said, staring at the blood. He gave Arlo and me a watery smile, then slumped to the ground.

"He's fine," Arlo said, taking my arm. "He just fainted. We have to keep moving. I need to get to Einar."

A loud roar echoed through the warehouse. More gunshots rang out.

"I think we found him," Arlo said grimly. "Come on." We ran toward the sound of the fighting, dodging debris and shattered statues. As we reached the end of the aisle, a vast production floor stretched before us. Daylight poured through a pair of busted metal doors, flooding the space.

A battle raged, the scene like something out of a fairy tale. Or maybe a nightmare. Everywhere I looked, mythical creatures fought werewolves. Centaurs galloped with swords in their hands, their biceps flexing as they slashed and parried. A giant crow swooped above the chaos. Rolfe romped in bear form among the werewolves, sending them flying with broad sweeps of his paws. Leander stood behind a stack of plastic crates, his head ablaze. Goliath crouched behind him. When a werewolf lunged at the crates, Leander swiped a handful of fire from his head and lobbed it at the wolf like a fiery baseball.

In the center of everything, Einar fought in hand-to-hand combat with a werewolf in human form. They grappled, fists swinging and sweat flying. The werewolf was huge, but Einar fought like a berserker, seemingly anticipating the path of the man's blows before they could land.

But something wasn't quite right. The next time Einar swung his fist, his muscles bulged, a bubble of flesh swelling from his skin. The werewolf ducked, then landed a vicious uppercut to Einar's ribs.

Einar staggered back. He snarled, his mouth full of too many teeth. Patches of fur dotted his skin. He was losing control.

"I have to help him," Arlo said. He disappeared, then reappeared next to Einar.

A whisper of sound behind me made me turn. Everything slowed down.

Armand leapt from the dust, his eyes bright gold and his fangs bared. I spun, my heart pounding, but he caught me and pulled me against his chest. Fingers scrabbled in my hair, and then wrenched my head to the side. Oh god, he was going to shoot me. As I drew breath to cry out, pain exploded in my neck. Hot liquid spilled down my shoulder. My mouth stretched on a soundless scream, and I realized he'd bitten me.

Somewhere in front of me, a broken, wrenching cry filled the air. It was the sound a wounded animal would make—sorrowful and gutting.

Pain engulfed me. Vaguely, I was aware of Armand releasing his bite. He shoved me away, and the ground reared up. I hit hard, striking my elbow, but the pain didn't register. The fire in my neck was too searing to make room for any other kind of discomfort.

Armand stepped around me, facing Einar across the warehouse with the gun in his hand. Everyone on both sides of the battle stilled, all eyes on Armand.

"I took her finger, Rothkilde!" Armand shouted. "Now I've taken her life. And you'll watch her die in agony."

Einar threw his head back and roared. His body contorted, the gruesome transformation overtaking him.

Pain and sorrow punched through me. We'd lost. Everything was lost. Blood spread in a pool under my bent legs. With an odd sort of detachment, I realized it was mine.

Goliath sprinted from behind Leander. He skidded to a halt halfway between Einar and Armand.

"You won't touch her!" he yelled, his shoulders heaving. The markings on his face glittered like emeralds. *Beautiful.* Goliath was beautiful. I should have told him when I had the chance.

Armand gave a cruel laugh. "I already did, runt. The bitch is dead. She just doesn't know it yet."

High overhead, a giant crow wheeled over the crowd, its wings spread as it wove in and out of the rafters. No one appeared to notice.

Tears streamed down Goliath's face. He balled his fists at

his sides as he glared at Armand. "You should have killed me when you had the chance."

The werewolves ranged around the warehouse laughed.

Armand aimed the gun at Goliath. "Good point. But better late than never, right? I'll do it now."

A crow's screech split the air.

Armand looked up as the crow plunged downward, plucking the gun from his hand.

Goliath exploded into a ball of fire. Around the warehouse, people cried out, ducking as the inferno roared twenty feet into the air. An enormous, green dragon rose from the flames. It flapped its wings, sending gusts of wind over the crowd. Rows of serrated teeth glittered like diamonds as the dragon opened its jaws and roared. The creature was glorious, from his emerald eyes to his lashing tail, which ended in a tuft of white, cotton candy fur.

Goliath. My heart lifted as the draft from his wings blew my hair back. His name fit better than I could have ever imagined.

He hovered in the air, his wings flapping and his narrowed eyes pinned on Armand. The werewolf staggered backward and almost fell.

"No!" he shouted, his voice high-pitched and frightened. "No, please!"

With a swift intake of oxygen, Goliath opened his jaws wide and spewed a stream of fire over Armand.

The crow screeched again, swooping from the sky. Myrna shifted in the air and stepped to the warehouse floor on two feet.

Armand screamed, his arms flailing as the fire consumed him. He staggered around, facing me. Skin melted down his face. His eyes went wide with terror. Then he dropped to the ground. Dead.

Goliath shot into the air, his wings spread wide and his

talons tucked close to his body. With terror-filled cries, wolves ran toward the daylight that spilled through the broken metal doors. Fire streaked through the air and roasted the wolves before they could escape.

The battle resumed. Leander jumped from behind the crates, pumping his fist and grinning as he watched Goliath decimate the werewolves. The tide had turned.

But Einar was out of control. Stuck in his monstrous half form, he struck out at his own people, sending a centaur crashing to the ground. Arlo grabbed at him, but Einar shook him off.

Arlo's words flowed through my memory. "*Fated mates are rare among lycans, but the histories tell of such matches occurring.*"

Pain consumed me. It spread from my neck through the rest of my body, every beat of my heart a new chapter in agony. As Einar continued to rage, I tried to stand. But my legs buckled, and I went back down.

So I crawled, memories of Einar flooding my mind.

"No one challenges me like you do. No one dares. Every time we argue, I walk away wondering if I should have kissed you instead."

"I don't hate humans. In fact, I find myself utterly entranced by this one."

"I want every drop of honey, sweetheart. Say yes."

"Yes," I said, my voice a whisper of sound. I clenched my teeth against a sudden chill that racked my bones.

Across the warehouse, foam flecked Einar's lips. He roared and slashed his claws at everyone who tried to get close to him.

I had to reach him. Cold crept through me, but I continued to crawl, grabbing at the floor and propelling myself forward. Spots danced in my vision.

Einar. I tried to say it, but my lips were numb.

He whirled toward me. And he stopped, his chest heaving. Raw flesh glistened between his exposed ribs. Chunks of fur sprouted across his body in patches, giving him the look of a dog with mange.

Pain seared me, but I kept crawling. After another second, I couldn't feel my legs. I had to reach him. I drew a deep breath.

"Einar!" My voice echoed in my ears, the syllables of his name rippling. "Come back to me."

Einar stared. His brow furrowed. Slowly, the madness left his eyes. In a blur of bone and flesh, he transformed. Suddenly, a buff-colored lycan stood before me, its golden eyes burning with intelligence. In another blur, Einar shifted to two legs. Nude, he rushed to me, collapsing on the ground and gathering me in his arms.

"Harper," he rasped, tears sheening his eyes. He held a shaking hand over my neck. "I...oh gods."

As the strength drained from my body, I reached up, just managing to brush my fingertips over his cheek. "Your eyes..." I whispered. "I like...the silver...best."

He grabbed my hand and kissed my fingertips. His tears splashed on my face, but I didn't feel them land.

"Harper," he said. "I love you."

I smiled even as the cold crept to my chest. "I love you, too." The cold reached my neck. Shadows clustered at the edges of my vision.

"Stay with me," Einar said, his tears falling faster. "You have to stay."

So cold. My teeth should have chattered. Instead, a curious sort of peace floated through me. Einar's face grew blurry. Sounds faded. I'd read somewhere that hearing was the last sense to go.

As the shadows took over, I drew one last breath. Because I had something important to say. I had to make sure Einar heard me.

"It was never the centaurs," I said. "It was you."

CHAPTER TWENTY-THREE

EINAR

Harper's eyes drifted shut. Blood stopped pumping from her ruined neck. Her body was cold. She was gone. She was fucking gone.

"No!" I cried, my throat aching. I gathered Harper to me, burying my face in her hair. "Gods, no."

The warehouse was still, everyone silent around me. Tears stung my eyes, and pain lodged in my chest. Was this what a broken heart felt like? Wherever Harper was going, I wanted to go too. I'd just found her, and now she'd been ripped away from me.

No. Fuck no. I wouldn't allow it.

I lifted my head. Blinking away tears, I spotted Adina in the crowd.

"Make a potion," I ordered. "You have to save her."

Adina moved forward, her expression stricken. "I know of no such potion, Prince Einar. Harper was bitten by a werewolf. Human females so rarely make the turn. And...Harper is already gone. If there's a potion to bring her back, I've never heard of it."

The ache in my chest intensified. Once again, helplessness gripped me. "What am I going to do?" I asked, unsure if I asked Adina or the crowd in general. Or maybe I asked myself. Not the gods, surely. They'd never answered my pleas before.

No, they'd cursed me. Punished me. Maybe that's what this was. I'd evaded their judgment once, escaping lycan society with my life after I took someone else's. Using my position and my brother's money, I'd fled across the country and built a prison I could tolerate.

And now the gods had caught up to me. They'd given me the perfect woman and then forced me to watch her die.

"Fuck off!" I snarled. Someone in the crowd gasped. They probably thought I was losing my mind for good. It didn't matter. Nothing mattered anymore.

"Sir."

I turned my head. Arlo knelt beside me, his human form bruised and slightly gaunt. That he bore any physical injuries at all meant Armand had hurt him badly. *My fault.* This was all my fault.

"I think I know a way to save her," Arlo said.

It took a second for his words to sink in. When they did, I latched onto them like a drowning man glimpsing the edge of the shore. "Tell me."

"The book."

My heart skipped a beat. He meant the Book of Crubeus. It would show me whatever knowledge my heart most desired.

Arlo nodded, clearly seeing the understanding in my eyes. "If you want this badly enough—if it's possible to bring her back—the book should show you a way."

My heart pumped faster. "Get it for me. Please." Of anyone alive, he was the most qualified to fetch it.

Arlo reached into the air and grasped the book. Murmurs

ran through the crowd, everyone likely seeing the book in a way that most appealed to them.

"You've never looked for this knowledge before," Arlo said, placing the book on the dusty concrete. "You should prepare for a battle."

I settled Harper gently on the ground, my heart catching at the sight of her grayish skin and torn neck. But she was still beautiful. Her strawberry blond hair spread around her, and her thick lashes lay like fans on her cheeks.

Whispers lifted from the book. Around me, the crowd moved forward, drawn to it.

"Stand back," Arlo said, his features sharpening. "This book is a predator, and you're all prey. It takes a great deal of training to resist its power."

A few people grumbled, but the crowd eased back.

I knelt and opened the book. Immediately, light blasted my vision, and words blazed on the page. Spells and incantations. Potions and curses. The lines shifted and rewrote themselves, offering knowledge. But it wasn't the kind I sought.

Harper. I want to save Harper.

The pages flipped, buffeted by an invisible wind. The warehouse fell away. The writing on the page gleamed more brightly. And then images replaced the words. I braced to see Harper.

Instead, I saw myself. Memories flickered before my eyes—each one showing me at various points in my life. Regrets and mistakes filled my vision.

Me as a child, glaring from the sidelines as my father taught Cyrus to hunt.

Me as a teenager, berating a weeping servant because she put too much starch in my shirts.

Me courting a lycan nobleman's daughter, only to break

things off when I grew bored. The images flashed more quickly, the woman replaced with another. And another.

The vision changed, and I stood before Cyrus, anger boiling inside me. "*Yes, my lord,*" I said, sweeping a mocking bow before slamming from his office. After I left, my brother stared at the door, sorrow in his eyes. He sat back in his chair and scrubbed a hand over his face. A rough sob leaked around his palm, and his shoulders slumped. The crown weighed on him. I'd never known. I hadn't been there to help him bear the burden. I'd been too consumed with myself—too prideful and arrogant to accept the love he offered.

"Focus," Arlo said from somewhere. "You need to focus on Harper."

The pages flipped, and Harper's life appeared. Her smile flashed as she tore through a newsroom, running past cubicles to reach her father's office. Her girlish pigtails bounced. Reporters leaned in their chairs, fond expressions on their faces as she passed.

The vision changed, and she smiled as she watched her mother interview a chef. Her mother caught Harper's eye and winked.

Another change, and now Harper bent over a spiral notebook, her tongue between her teeth as she scribbled down a story. The clock on the wall behind her showed the time as ten minutes past midnight.

The vision changed again. Harper sat hollow-eyed at her mother's bedside while a nurse moved around the room. Margaret stared straight at Harper and murmured, "Who are you?"

Who are you? The question rippled around me, the words growing louder. Lines of text bled down the book's pages, obscuring the vision of Harper and her mother.

Who are you?

Magic sparked against my skin, stinging as it struck.

I clenched my jaw. The book's pages flipped, and now each page displayed the same three words.

Who are you?

The words glowed. Whispers whipped around me, repeating the question over and over. The magic burned. Its embers sank into my skin. Burrowed into my veins. Burning. The old, familiar fire flared to life.

Who are you?

My beast thrashed inside me. For so long, I'd asked the book to restore me. To do what the gods would not and help me find a way to repair the rent in my soul.

Who are you?

Gritting my teeth, I answered with my gift. *"Einar Rothkilde!"* But that was my name. Nothing more. Who was I, really? Prince. Lycan. Criminal. Unworthy of forgiveness. I was all of those things.

Harper's face floated before me, her blue eyes shining with love.

Something wet touched my cheeks. I bent my head and let the tears fall faster. *"Forgive me."*

Words blazed from the page, knowledge hovering underneath them. But I couldn't reach it.

I extended my hand, straining toward the priceless knowledge. A red hand tipped with black claws burst through the center of the page and reached for me. It gripped my palm and tugged hard, dragging me forward. The stench of brimstone invaded my lungs.

Slowly, a potion wrote itself down the page. The words were foreign, but I understood them. Because they were for me. It was the potion to bring Harper back to life.

But the book demanded a price.

Who are you?

The book laughed, and its answer echoed through my head. *Einar Rothkilde, you are mine.*

Light spread. The hand gripping mine pulled me forward.

Arlo stepped into view, his body haloed by the light. Fully demonic, he hefted a long, black broadsword and bared his fangs. "I am King Crubeus's son and heir," he snarled. "And I command you to release Einar Rothkilde." He swung the sword, severing the clawed hand at the wrist.

I fell backward—and landed on my ass on the warehouse floor. The Book of Crubeus slammed shut, its light winking out.

Arlo stood a few feet away, his chest rising and falling as he caught his breath. The black sword was gone. There was no sign of the clawed hand.

Around us, people stared at Arlo with shocked expressions.

"You saved my life," I told him.

"You saved mine first," he said.

A lump formed in my throat. "I didn't."

One corner of his mouth lifted. "You don't think giving me a place to live and offering me friendship saved me? I assure you, it did." He came to me and put out a hand. When I grabbed it, he tugged me to my feet. "The human world didn't accept me fifty years ago," he said softly. "The demon plane doesn't accept me now. But you do. You always have."

I swallowed the impulse to argue, and I put a hand on his shoulder. "Thank you, old friend. But you didn't have to reveal yourself." Arlo could change his glamour, but his cover was blown. Now everyone knew my steward was the missing King of the Legerdemain.

"I was happy to do it," Arlo said. His shoulder lifted under my palm as he sighed. "I can't hide forever. And...a Scorab was here. It's a long story, but he recognized me."

Worry swirled through me. Arlo's father had been dead for

half a century. But the laws of the Legerdemain were clear. Arlo was heir to the throne. While he lived, no one else could rule. His people didn't want him for their king, but they couldn't pick a new one until he was dead. The Legerdemain were unlikely to try killing him outright. But they might send someone from a different demon clan to rid themselves of a king they were too bigoted and narrow-minded to accept.

I looked at the book. "It listened to you." I turned back to Arlo. "That was a ballsy move, stepping into my vision." It went against all the advice Arlo had given me over the years. Demons didn't share their plane with humans, and their world was steeped in magic. Like all demonic artifacts, the book's magic was potent and unpredictable. Arlo had taught me how to resist it over the years. The key was to read in short bursts, like ingesting small sips of poison to build up a tolerance.

A faint smile touched Arlo's lips. "To be honest, I wasn't sure that was going to work. My father created the book. He was the only one capable of defying it. I took a risk that it would listen to me as his heir." He looked at Harper on the ground. "She taught me that some risks are worth taking, no matter how shitty the odds."

I went to Harper and knelt beside her. Then I looked around and caught Adina's eye. "I have the potion in my head. If I tell you the ingredients, can you make it?"

She nodded, and her voice was breathless as she said, "I can try. But I'll need my cauldron."

I looked at Arlo.

He nodded. "I'll get it. And anything else we need."

Adina crossed to me and knelt on Harper's other side. She smoothed a tendril of strawberry blond hair off Harper's forehead. Then she lifted her gaze to mine.

"Tell me the potion, Your Highness. I'll help you bring her back."

CHAPTER TWENTY-FOUR

HARPER

Something smelled amazing.

I moved through my parents' house, my nose leading me to the kitchen. The appliances gleamed, everything clean and sparkling. Mom stood at the stove with her back to me. Steam rose in lazy curls from an array of pots.

For some reason, tears stung my eyes. I pressed my lips together, my heart pumping wildly.

Mom turned and caught my gaze. "Oh, there you are, Harper! Dinner is almost ready, but I wanted to show you something first." She wiped her hands on a towel, then crossed the kitchen and took my face in her hands. Her brow furrowed as she swiped cool thumbs under my eyes. "Are you crying?"

"No," I said through a thick throat. "Just hungry, I think."

She smiled, her eyes twinkling. "Well. We'll fix that in a minute. Come on." She slipped her hand into mine. "I can't wait to show you this new piece I just bought."

Hand in hand, we went to the foyer. Sunlight streamed through the windows, casting a glow over the furniture. Mom went to her curio cabinet and opened the doors. Withdrawing a small, delicate vase decorated with two scrolling handles, she faced me.

"The glassblower just delivered it today. It's a priceless piece. One of a kind, really. But it was broken before." Mom shrugged and gave a good-natured laugh. "Well, it'll always be broken, I guess. You can see the repair where the handle attaches."

I moved closer, peering at the spot she indicated. "Yeah...I see it."

Mom sighed. "It's still beautiful, though." She looked at me and smiled. "The whole piece is stronger now. And the glass-blower found an additional crack when he was working. So, in a way, maybe it was a good thing the handle was broken."

My breath caught. My heart pumped faster. The sunlight grew stronger, swelling so much it obscured the furniture around us.

Mom's smile turned impossibly gentle. "Sometimes, the broken pieces are the strongest. We can't really fix them. But it doesn't matter. They're still beautiful."

Tears ran down my cheeks. I put a trembling palm over my mouth.

My mother came to me and took my hands. The vase was gone. The foyer shimmered, the light so bright it should have stung my eyes. Mom gleamed in the center of it, her body somehow brighter than the sun.

"I'm so sorry, baby, but you can't stay," she said, her voice wrapping around me like a hug. She squeezed my hands. "You have a very important story to write."

I swallowed. "Which story?"

Mom leaned forward and kissed my forehead. "Yours."

I opened my eyes on a gasp. Einar smiled down at me, his head wreathed with light and...dust?

The battle rushed back. We were still in the warehouse. I

lay in his lap, my head cradled in the crook of his elbow. Around us, a raucous cheer went up. As my eyes focused, I turned my head and caught glimpses of people hugging and celebrating. Everyone from the maze was present, their faces full of joy. My father appeared at the edge of the crowd. Tears streamed down his face. One of the centaurs trotted over to him and put an arm around Dad's shoulders.

Myrna stood off to the side, a smile shining in her eyes. Then she squawked as Leander spun her into his arms and planted a loud kiss on her cheek. Rolfe and Goliath embraced, Goliath's smaller form swallowed by Rolfe's bulk. A smiling Keir caught my eye and offered a gentlemanly bow.

A short distance away, Adina stood with Arlo. The bog witch nudged Arlo, a smug look on her face. "Told you they were fated mates."

Arlo sighed, reached into his back pocket, and handed her money.

Einar touched my cheek, drawing my gaze back to him.

"What happened?" I croaked.

Einar smiled. "You tamed the beast."

Joy and disbelief soared through me, threatening to lift me from his arms and toss me into the sky. And I could have done it. I felt...good. Better than good, actually, my body free from pain. I lifted my right hand—and my happiness faded at the sight of my severed pinky. The skin was healed, but the end of my finger was gone.

"It's okay," Einar said, wrapping his fingers around mine and holding my hand against his heart. "If it bothers you, we'll find a way to fix it. But I promise you with all my heart, it doesn't bother me." His heart thumped against my hand as if it wanted to echo his vow.

I drew a deep breath, Adina's talk of fated mates ringing in my mind. "Are we...mated?"

"We are," Einar murmured. He kissed my knuckles. "You're a lycan now. We're bound until our stories end."

Tears burned my throat as my mother's words overlapped with Einar's. A little voice in my head told me to kiss him now and ask questions later, but I couldn't muffle the spark of curiosity that flared to life inside me. "How did you make this happen?"

"You remember the book you saw on my desk?"

I nodded. "The one that shows you whatever knowledge your heart desires."

"That's right. I've read it often over the years, searching for a way to gain control of my beast. But I was looking for the wrong thing. And something tells me I'll never find a way to fix what's broken inside me. You tamed my beast, but I'm still a rogue. That's okay, though. I finally found what I was looking for."

Now, the tears trickled from my eyes and slid into my hair. And my nose ran, which was probably unsexy, but who cared?

I sniffed, smiling through my tears. "What did you find?"

Einar drew a fingertip over the bridge of my nose, his silver eyes shining with love. "You're a reporter, Harper. Haven't you figured it out by now?" He bent, his mouth aiming for mine. Just before he kissed me, he whispered against my lips.

"You."

EPILOGUE

HARPER

A lycan was chasing me. But I wanted to be caught.

Happiness burst inside me as I flew through the forest on four feet. The wind whistled in my ears and whipped through my fur. Snow flew under my paws.

Tree branches snapped behind me. I laughed, and the sound emerged as a short, high-pitched bark. Einar wasn't even trying to be quiet.

I glanced back, and awe shivered through me at the sight of his golden eyes and powerful form. He was magnificent, every inch of his body rippling with muscle. After four months together, his shifts from man to lycan were smooth and nearly effortless.

But as he'd predicted, the fire hadn't left him. Einar was still a rogue. But our mate bond was an anchor that banked the fire. When the flames threatened, I pulled him into our bedroom and reminded him that he was loved. That it was okay to be less than perfect. I wasn't perfect, either. My anxiety disorder had returned with me from the edge of death. Apparently, some things just couldn't be fixed.

But that didn't mean they weren't beautiful.

The wind shifted. Einar's panting breaths grew closer. Anticipation buzzed in my veins as I burst into a clearing. A second later, Einar pounced.

We tumbled to the ground together, rolling over and over through the snow. My laughter started out as a series of barks and then slid into a human giggle as we shifted from four legs to two. And then Einar was on top of me, his thigh sliding between my legs and his smile curving against my neck.

"You lost that race on purpose," he murmured, reaching down and stroking the place between my legs that made me see stars.

"Are you complaining?" I asked, letting my eyes flutter shut as I arched against him. Moisture flooded me. My clit burned with need.

Einar continued working his magic, his fingers sending waves of pleasure through me. "No, not complaining," he whispered, trailing hot kisses along my jawline. "But now that I caught you, I get to claim my prize." He drew back, grasped my hips, and flipped me onto my stomach. Before I could get my bearings, he pulled me onto all fours and plunged inside me.

My pleasured cry echoed around the clearing. I dug my fingers into the snow as he began to thrust, his cock nudging my womb. The cold would have been intolerable before, but it didn't bother me now. Lycans were hot-blooded—a trait that was taking me a while to get used to. Even in the depths of winter, I spent most of my time in tank tops and shorts. Einar spent most of his time finding excuses to take them off me.

His fingers dug into my hips. A second later, a *crack* split the air, and pain flared over my ass.

My gasp was loud in the clearing as I met his gaze over my shoulder. "You did *not* just spank me."

A wicked light entered his silver eyes. "Don't even try to pretend you didn't like it, sweetheart. Your pussy just clamped so hard, I think I might lose circulation in my dick."

My cheeks heated. Einar chuckled. Then he fucked me harder, bending over me and licking the shell of my ear.

"I love those blushes," he rumbled in my ear. "And you want to know a secret?"

"Yes," I gasped, moving with him.

"When your cheeks turn pink, your pretty nipples do too. And I love it, Harper. I love seeing my wife flushed and breathless. I especially love knowing I made her that way."

Wife. I never got tired of hearing him say it. We'd married a month after the battle at the warehouse, the ceremony held at the entrance to the maze with Arlo officiating and all of Draithmere's inhabitants around us. Arlo insisted he wasn't concerned about the Legerdemain trying to assassinate him, but Einar and I still worried. After everything he'd done for us, Arlo deserved happiness.

In the meantime, he had his hands full helping my father repair my parents' house. The two of them had struck up an unlikely friendship, and now Arlo spent a few days a week in Seattle, working with Dad to make the property livable. Although, I suspected Einar sent Arlo to make sure my father had truly turned over a new leaf and didn't plan on writing any stories about the supernatural world.

Einar delivered another stinging slap to my ass, and my thoughts dissolved as my arousal flared hotter. Goosebumps lifted on my skin. I thrust my ass higher, offering Einar a better target.

My husband chuckled—and then his chuckle turned into a growl as I squeezed my inner muscles around him. He tangled a hand in my hair and tugged my head back, holding me steady as he pumped his hips faster.

My body rocked wildly in the snow. Dirt curled between my fingers. My breasts swayed, my nipples tight and aching. The scent of leather and pine flooded my lungs. I cried out as my orgasm rushed toward me.

Einar reached a hand under my body and found my clit. Two strokes was my undoing. My orgasm hit, and I screamed Einar's name as I came apart, my body shaking.

He followed a second later, his bellow bouncing off the trees as he pumped his hot release inside me. Then, gasping, he pulled out and collapsed in the snow with me in his arms.

We lay quietly for a few moments, our hearts beating in sync. A smile tugged at my lips as I deliberately tuned out the sound—a trick Einar had taught me so I didn't get overstimulated by too much noise. Heightened senses were cool, but I didn't need to hear Leander stumbling to the bathroom after a long night of drinking Adina's hard cider.

When Einar's breathing was even, I turned in his arms and stroked the golden stubble on his cheek. "Do you feel less nervous about meeting Cyrus this afternoon?"

My husband scowled. "I'm not nervous."

"Einar."

The scowl lingered a few more seconds. Then Einar sighed, a sheepish expression stealing over his rugged features. "Have I been that obvious?"

"A little," I said, smiling. I feathered my thumb over his jaw. "You have nothing to worry about. I'll be with you. And I've talked to Abby a lot over the phone and email. I think she and I are going to have a great time together."

The scowl reappeared. "More like scheme together. My brother has no idea what he's about to unleash."

I couldn't help my laugh. "Oh, I think he knows." I kissed the corner of Einar's mouth. "And if he's half as stubborn as you are, he deserves it."

SEVERAL HOURS LATER, NERVES GRIPPED ME AS I STOOD IN Draithmere's foyer with Einar at my side. Through the windows, a black sedan crawled up the driveway, its tires crunching in the snow. Out of habit, I tucked my right hand behind my back.

Einar caught my wrist, pulling my attention to him. My breath hitched as he lifted my severed pinky to his lips and kissed it.

"You look absolutely radiant in that dress, Harper Rothkilde," he murmured, tenderness shimmering in his eyes. "It's not fair, really. Brains and beauty in one fuckable package."

A snort escaped me before I could stop it. "Fuckable?"

He shrugged, a playful smile on his lips. "I just call them as I see them. You're the wordsmith around here." He leaned in and brushed a kiss on my cheek. "And my favorite author."

"I'm not an author yet," I said. But maybe someday... Working as a reporter was out of the question, even though I had every intention of finishing my degree. At first, I'd expected it to bother me. Growing up, I always assumed I would follow in my parents' footsteps.

But spending all those nights writing alone in my room had sparked something inside me. Facts were fine, but maybe fiction suited me better. And goodness knew my new life offered plenty of inspiration.

"You will be," Einar said breezily. "My favorite fuckable author."

My shoulders shook. I slapped his arm. "Excuse me, do you plan on having more than one?"

"No. My heart is yours." He slanted me a lascivious look. "Along with the rest of me."

We fell silent as the car stopped outside. Arlo exited and

went to the passenger door. Seconds later, a black-haired version of my husband approached the house. A beautiful woman walked at his side, her dark hair loose around her shoulders and a chubby baby in her arms. A little boy raced ahead of them, his small legs pumping.

"Max!" the man called out. "No running!"

The boy spun, dancing in place. "I'm not running, Daddy! I'm sprinting!"

Einar snorted. "Little shit," he said under his breath. He raised a brow at me. "Sounds like you're not the only one with a thesaurus."

I laced my fingers through his. Seconds later, Arlo led King Cyrus and his family into the foyer—and Einar faced his brother for the first time in ninety years.

For a moment, neither man said anything. They stared at each other, their matching silver eyes filled with wariness...and maybe a hint of fear.

Just when the silence stretched too long, Max, Cyrus's five-year-old son, walked up to Einar. The little boy cocked his head to the side and gave my husband an appraising look.

"Are you really my uncle?"

Einar cleared his throat. He stared at the boy, then crouched so his face was on Max's level. "Yes. Your father and I are brothers."

Max seemed to think this over. Then he leaned closer to Einar and lowered his voice. "I have a sister. She's okay, I guess."

Amusement shimmered in Einar's eyes. He looked at Abby, who seemed to fight a smile. The baby in her arms blinked, her wide blue eyes landing on Arlo.

He winked at her, and she rewarded him with a gummy smile.

Einar offered Max a sage nod. "Sisters can be all right once you get to know them. Brothers too." A muscle jumped in his jaw. "Family is important. One of the most important things, actually."

Abby pressed the fingers of her free hand to her lips. Tears gleamed in her eyes as she looked at Cyrus.

"That's true," he said, his deep voice laced with emotion. "Family is everything. Both the kind we're born into"—he looked at Arlo—"and the kind we choose."

My throat burned. Oh, god, I was going to cry and embarrass myself.

Einar straightened. I took his hand, then tugged him forward until we stood before Cyrus. Drawing on the YouTube tutorials I'd watched over the past few days, I dipped into what I hoped was a passable curtsy.

"It's an honor to have you in our home, my lord. You and Queen Abby and your beautiful family are very welcome."

"No," Cyrus murmured, putting a hand under my elbow and pulling me upright. "You never bow to anyone, Harper." He lifted my hand and brushed a respectful kiss over my knuckles. "It's *my* honor to meet the woman who brought my brother back to me."

Einar sucked in a breath. He locked gazes with Cyrus. They moved at the same time, throwing their arms around each other. After a moment, Einar nodded, and it was obvious they spoke mind-to-mind.

Abby came to my side. Max moved with her, hugging his mother's leg and staring up at me with eyes the same color as King Cyrus's—and my husband's.

"Is it true that a werewolf chopped your pinky off?"

"Max!" Abby cried. She turned to me, her face a mask of horror. "I am *so* sorry, Harper. I can't believe he said that." She looked at her son. "Maximilian Rothkilde, you and I are going to have words, young man."

"It's okay," I said. I stuck out my right hand, letting Max have a look. "Yep. He cut it off with a knife. But it's all better now."

Max's eyes filled with awe. He looked up at me, hero worship on his face. "That is bad ass, Aunt Harper."

"Max!" Abby said.

I laughed, joy spreading through me. As Einar, Cyrus, and Arlo joined us, I grinned at my new family. "You're right," I told Max. "It's pretty bad ass."

About Amy Pennza

Amy Pennza is a USA Today Bestselling Author of steamy fantasy romance. After stints as a lawyer and a soldier, she discovered her dream job is writing dirty, swoony books. She lives in the Great Lakes region with her husband and five children.

Keep up with new releases by visiting amypennza.com

Sign up for Amy's newsletter and get a FREE scorching-hot paranormal romance!
www.amypennza.com/subscribe

ALSO BY AMY PENNZA

Check out all my books by visiting my Amazon author page or my website.

The Royal Lycans Series:

The Lycan King's Captive

Prisoner of the Lycan Prince

The Bitten and Bound Series. Dark Fantasy MMF Menage:

Given

Stolen

Kept

The Dragon Lairds Series. Paranormal Romance MMF Menage:

Kiss of Smoke

Dark Fire Kiss

Kiss of a Dragon King

Kiss of Frost

Kiss of Embers

Lux Catena Wolf Shifters Series:

What a Wolf Desires

What a Wolf Dares

What a Wolf Demands

What a Wolf's Heart Decides

Made in the USA
Monee, IL
05 July 2025

20400494R00166